With Angel Tanner, the android that runs California's criminal underworld, pulling the strings, PI Cassie Tam finds herself thrust into a conflict with New Hopeland's biggest and baddest. But working with the murderous AI may be the only way that Cassie can get to the bottom of her home's greatest mystery: What *is* New Hopeland City?

As she struggles to balance her dealings with allies and enemies alike, Cassie is left with a difficult choice. She has always straddled the line between light and dark. Now, the time to decide which side she's on is drawing close...*if* she can figure out which is which.

HALF LIGHT

The Cassie Tam Files, Book Five

Matt Doyle

A NineStar Press Publication

Published by NineStar Press
P.O. Box 91792,
Albuquerque, New Mexico, 87199 USA.
www.ninestarpress.com

Half Light

Printed in the USA
First Edition
March, 2020

Print ISBN: 978-1-951880-62-0

Also available in eBook, ISBN: 978-1-951880-62-0

Warning: This book is part of a series and needs to be read in sequence. It contains violence, guns, and mentions of past executions of women and children.

Chapter One

"*Diu.*"

I look to my right and find a free space to pull the car into. I have a couple of different ringtones on my cell phone, each assigned to give me a clear idea of whether I need—or want—to answer it. This generic-but-far-too-loud melody marks this call as coming from one particular number. Given what day it is, I've been expecting to hear from them. The last few days have been spent playing a game that's essentially the adult equivalent of passing notes in class. I leave a note somewhere, I get another at home, I respond somewhere else. It's been a pain, and it's all been leading up to this. "It's where it leads next I'm worried about."

I steel myself and tap the screen to answer the call. A female voice comes through, dripping with an overacted panic. "Is…is that Cassandra Tam?"

I recognise the voice instantly. "It is. Cassie or Caz is fine."

"My name is Anna Welch. I need help, Miss Tam."

I sigh. "Well, that's what I'm here for. Do you want to discuss this over the phone, or would you rather meet in person?"

"In person," she replies, and I can hear the smile in her voice. "Somewhere neutral would be best. I'm rather paranoid, you see."

"Okay, that's fine. Where?"

"I'll text you the location."

She hangs up, and the text comes through almost immediately. Once I've finished reading it, I can't help but smile. She wants to meet at an old abandoned warehouse. It's one I'm familiar with. A few months back, I broke up a dog fight in the same building. During the case, I discovered there's a secret entrance to the building via an underground network of hallways. *That* gives me a way to monitor her if I need to. Or a convenient escape route.

I hit the speed dial for Lori, and it goes straight to her answering service. After the beep, I say, "Hey, it's Cassie. I guess you're driving. Listen, I've just had a call from a potential client, and I'm gonna have to go meet with them. I'm still coming, but it may be worth checking what later times there are for the film, just in case this runs long. Anyway. Be with you soon."

I throw my phone onto the passenger seat next to me and pull out into the light traffic of the New Hopeland afternoon.

*

By the time I reach the warehouse, I've already run through a number of different scenarios in my head. None of them ended well, so I'm putting my faith in reality right now. "No fear, Tam, this was a voluntary trip," I remind myself, and push the main door open. Inside looks the same as it did the last time I was here, minus the boxed area. And people.

Frowning, I make my way towards the back of the building and start checking doors. Finally, I spot a far-too-tight black ponytail, illuminated by the screen of a computer. "Welch. Real cute using the surname of the woman you murdered," I say, just loud enough to make sure she heard it.

Angel Tanner spins in her chair towards me and laughs, casually turning her monitor off as she does so. "Now, detective, you know full well Harold did that."

"The way I understand it, it amounts to much the same thing, eh?" I walk into the room and she rises to meet me. When she offers a handshake, I take it on instinct.

"Actually, no. The core result is the same, but the *point* is it wasn't me. That makes it a *very* different thing, at least in the eyes of the law. Still, I'm happy you reached out."

"I almost didn't," I say and then shake my head. "No, that's not true. I considered looking for a different way to contact you after I found out our *mutual acquaintance* was Gary Locke. You could have got in touch any time you wanted."

"Yes, I could have. But I knew talking to Mister Locke would be hard for you after that whole unfortunate incident with your girlfriend and her brother."

"Unfortunate incident?" I reply, my words dripping with a mix of anger and shock. "He tried to kill both of us. And he convinced her brother to take his own life for a cause that wasn't even real."

"Which is why I did it this way. I needed to know you were serious in your intention. Oh, and the cause was real, I'm certain of that. Or the part Locke cared about was anyway."

I grunt and shake my head. "I didn't come here to talk about conspiracy theories. You said I wanted to know what's happening in New Hopeland, and you're right. You want help to find out the same thing, so I came. Can we please get on with this? I have plans."

She smiles her creepy smile and nods. "You and me both, detective. But that's fine. Today was more about checking you're on board than anything. So, this will be our base of operations for the time being. It's out of the way, and it's neither used nor monitored, so it's fit for purpose."

I shrug. "Seems okay. It's easy enough to get to."

"I should hope so. You'll be spending a good amount of time here. Now, to business. What I said on the phone wasn't entirely false; I really do need your help. As you can imagine, I can't move freely right now, and my links in the city aren't particularly well suited for certain jobs. Like the one I have for you to do tomorrow."

"Which is?"

She pulls an envelope out of her pocket and hands it to me. "This contains a couple of photographs relating to *Anna Welch's* case. You're going to visit Mister Locke at the prison tomorrow morning and question him about them. They contain some gifts for him, a mild drug on one, and a special communicator on the other. You'll find a corresponding communicator in there, too, along with instructions as to what to do with it. Make sure you read them somewhere cameras can't see them clearly."

"Great. You know, he wasn't happy to see me the last time."

"I don't doubt it. Harold will make sure he plays nice though. I trust you can do the same?"

"For now."

"Good enough." She waves me away and heads back to her computer. "Now, go enjoy yourself. We'll talk more soon."

Play nicely. Follow orders until you know more. I leave without another word.

*

I put the knife down on the chopping board and giggle as Lori nervously glances towards a sound outside. "I'm sorry, but it's normally me who gets scared. You're the one who's supposed to be protecting me from the monsters on screen."

"I can't help it," Lori says, her tone almost indignant. "Goats...really freak me out."

I lean back against the counter and tilt my head, showing her a playful frown. "Then why go to a film about the Maryland Goatman?"

"Because *you* wanted to see it."

"Nuh-uh, you don't get to shift that one to me. You were definitely into seeing it too."

"I didn't think it would be *so* scary. He's part man, I thought that would counteract the goat bit. Plus, we didn't really see him in the trailer, so I wasn't expecting...*that,*" she replies, waving her hand in a vaguely Goatman shape.

"He did look good," I say and return to chopping a carrot.

"Effective, not good," Lori says and fires up the hob. She throws a couple of steaks into a pan, and the oil immediately starts to sizzle noisily.

"So, what is it with goats?" I ask.

"That's my gran's fault. I had this stuffed troll when I was little. It used to come with me on sleepovers. Eddie and I were staying at our grandparents' place one weekend, and when she saw it, she said she knew a bedtime story about a troll."

I smile. It's good Lori is able to mention her brother's name without the clear pain now. Plus, I like hearing about her childhood. She had far fewer scuffles than I did. *Wait. Trolls. Goats.* "She told you the story of the *Three Billy Goats Gruff*?"

Lori shivers. "Exactly."

"I'm not sure I follow."

"Those goats were bullies. They wanted to trespass on the troll's field, and when he quite rightly said no, one of them pushed him into the river and killed him."

"I'm not sure that's how most kids take the story, you know."

"I really loved trolls as a kid. And my one, he used to keep the nightmares away. So, the thought of these terrifying monsters who could kill a troll, just like that...Urgh."

I giggle again because I can't help it, and Lori taps me on the head with the fork she's using to keep the meat moving. "Don't you laugh at me, Miss Hides-from-everything-other-than-goats. They scream like people, too, you know. That's just plain creepy."

I scrape the carrots into a steamer and make a start on the tomatoes, struggling to keep from laughing again. "Well, what about that guy at the TS meets? Jerry? He's a goat."

"No, he's Jerry. Even in his gear, you can see him in there. Besides, Ink isn't afraid of goats."

"What about gargoyles?"

Lori smiles and adds some spice to the pan. "Isn't it more of an issue if he's scared of me?"

"True. Still, I do think Bert knows you well enough to recognise you. Plus, he didn't react badly to Donal O'Brien in his TS gear."

"Bert's sweet; I trust him not to go nuts on me. I still think it's a good idea to not introduce us at a meet though. So many unfamiliar Tech Shifters in the same place? It could spook him. Especially with how far into their headspace some of them go."

"Yeah, I think you're right. Maybe we could give it a try early next week?"

"Sure. How do you want yours, by the way?"

I glance over and she nods into the pan. "Well done. What else should I cut up for the salad? I don't want to leave you foodless."

"I've got plenty in. If you check the fridge, there should be some mushrooms and peppers. Maybe some lettuce too?"

"I'm on it. You ever cook onions in with the steaks? They really soak up the juices."

"Sounds good. There's a bag of prechopped onion in there. If you could grab it, I'll throw a handful in."

I hand over the bag and return to my chopping board. This time, I take two plates and start serving up the food as I go. "Wine or coffee?"

"Coffee, I think. It'll stave off the nightmares a bit longer. You know, it's a shame the restaurant was closed. Just our luck to finally get a reservation for the day they flood, right? Cooking together is fun though."

"I could really get used to this." The moment the words leave my mouth, I automatically hit panic mode and start babbling in an effort to stall on saying what I want to but am too scared to. "Cooking together, I mean. It's fun, you're right. Hey, wanna find something on TV in a minute? To take your mind off the Goatman?"

Lori smiles gently and gives me an even gentler kiss on the forehead before sliding a steak onto each plate. "Sounds good. And for the record, I could get used to it too."

*

"Still working the same case?" the guard asks.

The last time I visited Gary Locke was to push the Angel Tanner connection, and the same guard had accompanied me then. I fed him a line about working a case linked to one of Gary's old associates, which wasn't a complete lie but seemed to satisfy him. Looks like he remembers.

I nod. "Yeah. I managed to find some new evidence and wanted to see how he reacts to it. I'm hoping he'll give me something a little more on this occasion."

"It didn't seem like he said much last time," the guard comments. "I guess he's still sore about you getting him locked up."

"Probably."

"Well, expect him to be in a bad mood. He had a bit of a run-in with another prisoner last night."

"Oh? Anyone I know?"

To my surprise, the guard scratches his chin and gives me an answer other than *that's confidential.* "Yes, actually. Harold Sanderson. I hadn't thought of that until you mentioned it. You were working on that vampire case with the police, right?"

Diu. *Well, no sense in lying now. Let's try shifting him from suspicion to something else.* "Yeah. Maybe they had an argument over who I screwed the most?"

He laughs. "Maybe. Which do you think you did?"

I shrug. "Sanderson, I guess? I shot him three times. Locke, I only shot once, eh?"

"Well, in a way, Sanderson is lucky Locke is in poor health in general. Even being kept away from the stimulants and VR, I think he's done enough damage to his body that he'll never fully recover. With the bullet wounds, it's going to be a while before Sanderson is at his physical best. Right now, Locke's probably the biggest he could comfortably take."

"It sounds like you think about prisoners fighting a lot."

"Only because they *do* fight a lot."

We reach the door to the private interview room, and the guard places his hand on the door. "Same as last time. There are two cameras, so we'll be keeping an eye on things. If he tries anything, there's a panic button under your side of the table."

I nod, and he lets me in.

The interview room is pretty barren. I don't know if the cameras capture audio, but their angles mean they'll definitely pick up lip movements. So, keeping up the charade of being here about the case is important.

Sitting at the far end of a small table, his hands in cuffs, is Gary Locke.

"M-Miss Tam," he wheezes. "So nice to see you again."

"Sure, it is," I reply and take the seat opposite him. I nod towards his visibly taped side and add, "Looks like Harold Sanderson did a number on you."

"Just a cracked rib and a stiff jaw. It's my own fault really. Still, M-Mister Sanderson did say something interesting. Tell me, how i-is Lori? Given *your* history, I'm not sure Eddie would have approved."

I ball one hand into a fist and grit my teeth. "If it weren't for my client, you'd be regretting that already."

He laughs, and it's full of the same confidence he had on the night he was arrested. He thought he held all the cards then. This time, he really does. For now, at least. "Remind me to thank y-your client then. Now, what do you want?"

The ruse Angel has set up is a simple one, which is good, as the more complicated the lie, the harder it is to make it work. So, I pull two photos out of the envelope and push them towards Gary. "The woman is my client, Anna Welch. The men are who I'm interested in."

He grins. "Aww, d-does Lori know? She'll be so upset."

Not one to be outdone, I return the smile and lock my gaze with his. It's amazing how much you can convey with your eyes if you're properly motivated. "Keep pushing it."

Gary's grin drops instantly. He lets out a nervous cough and drops his gaze to the photos. When he picks the first one up, he starts subtly scraping a fingernail over the bottom right corner on the back of the print. His nails are surprisingly well kept, meaning nobody is going to notice the white residue he's gathering as he scrapes. According to the notes Angel gave me, it's a sickness inducing drug, cut with a small sample of the stimulant Gary is addicted to.

Gary sniffs in a bored manner and chucks the photo back to me and then picks up the other one. He gives it a look-over and then glances back to me and says, "Don't know them."

"See, I think you do. You noticed their shirts, right?"

Gary rolls his eyes and starts absently peeling a small sticker off the back of the print. "Of course, I did. The Roots of Eden are Rotten died as a movement with the website, M-Miss Tam. You made sure of it. The cause though? Clearly, *that* at least carries on."

"I'm not sure I believe you."

"I'm sure you don't. But you do know how easy it is to create a T-shirt. The site had decent traffic. These are clearly j-just fans who either enjoyed the content or wanted to continue to fight. Let me guess. Y-your client is in a position of power?"

I shrug. "You *could* say that."

"Then she is undoubtedly hiding something."

"We all have things to hide, Mister Locke. But nothing stays hidden forever. If you're hiding knowledge of who these two men are, that won't look good for you when I report it to the PD."

Gary curls his lip into a sneer and pushes the photo back to me with a snort. He stands up, quickly pressing the sticker to the side of his prison garb, and then looks to the door and yells, "Hey. We're done here. Take me back to my cell."

The guard opens the door and looks to me. I give a less than satisfied nod and gather the photos back up.

*

Angel's instructions were very clear. So, come the early afternoon, I headed to my bathroom and gave my hair a wash. She hadn't asked me to do anything other than go to the bathroom, but I felt like my hair needed it, so why not. Once I was done, I stuck a small earpiece in my ear and pulled out another sticker like the one Locke took. On the back was a transmitter. Looking at it now, it's remarkably small. According to the papers that came in the envelope, I'm supposed to place in the roof of my mouth, and it'll act like a microphone and receiver, wirelessly transmitting the received audio to the earpiece. My guess is Angel is linked up to this, too, and will be hearing every word.

I sigh and carefully remove the transmitter from the sticker and then open my mouth and press it in just behind my teeth. The tiny needles built into the thing pinch as they embed themselves, and once locked in place, the device emits a small buzz to let me know it's working. "Okay," I say. "Let's do this."

As instructed, I leave the bathroom in silence and start doing some housework. Within moments, Gary's voice comes through in the earpiece, albeit a little quietly.

"Good, everything is working. I apologise for having to keep my voice low. The drug worked; though I wasn't expecting blood to come up with the vomit. Regardless, I'm in the private cell in the infirmary, but they still listen. If I'm under the covers, I can talk without being noticed. Can you still hear?"

Angel's voice cuts in, confirming my suspicions. "Cassie, remain silent. If you can hear him fine, click your tongue." I do so, and Angel continues, "We can both hear you fine. Now, what do you have to offer?"

"Information, M-Miss Tanner. As I understand it, you want to know more about New Hopeland's history. Or the side of it the public records don't reflect. Before M-Miss Tam had me placed in here, I had access to *a lot* of things that may interest you."

"Summarise," she says.

"Let's start with New Hopeland's most famous creation, Tech Shift gear. The technology has been available to the public for five years now, but it was first conceived some time before that as part of a much larger initiative. In fact, it was referenced in the original plans for the current police station. I would not be surprised if there weren't other similar government contracts; ones that were in place long before they became public knowledge. Or in some cases, contracts destined to never be made available to the public. Much of my research was based on following the breadcrumbs on that basis.

"For example, if you were to contract several small companies, all of whom are run by the same few people, and ask them to produce small parts for use in different items, do you know what you could do? Build secret technology into seemingly innocuous items. Video and audio transmitters were the obvious ones, but I understand you already discovered one of the bigger projects. Who would have thought a simple environmental system like the EU25s could house holographic projectors?"

He's talking about the roadside air processors used to clean up emissions from the city's non-electric vehicles. Who would have thought the conspiracy nuts crying about them being something more sinister than high-end air cleaners were on to something?

"Based on what I dug up, the EU25s were in planning for a long time, though there was no set date for them to be released. My guess is they were either ready earlier than planned, or something caused the need for them to exist sooner. With the number of small parts contracts funnelled into them, though, it should have been clear they weren't entirely what they seemed. And there's evidence of a lot more of these modifications, especially with the TS gear. Like I said, you just have to follow the breadcrumbs. Most people don't because the government crows eat them up before anyone can spot them."

"And can you prove any of this, or is it all just wild theories?" Angel asks.

"I have evidence, though I hadn't finished going through it all. Piecing it together was a team effort before *The Roots of Eden are Rotten* was shut down. I already t-told Sanderson my price for this. I want out of this place."

"If you can provide me with proof of what you're saying, even if it's incomplete, I will make sure you get what you want."

"Give me what I want, and I'll give you the information."

"I see. I would rather not be starting from a near blank slate but knowing what I need to look for is enough of a start point. Goodbye, Mister Locke."

"No, wait," he says, far too quickly. Clearly, he expected his little show of bravado to work far better than it did.

"I'm listening."

"I'll tell you where I stored everything."

"Okay, better."

Gary sighs. "Everything is backed up on a memory stick. It's stored in the wishing well at the park near Main Street. Not in the well itself. There's a loose brick at the bottom. Lift that, and dig. Just don't use the stick on anything connected to a New Hopeland system, as the contents of the files will be picked up on the regular government scans."

"How did you access them when you needed to?"

"I used a modified NHC Blend phone. There should still be one with the stick, but if it's broken, there are always options. T.J. Crest Repairs is a few blocks from the park. Go there and speak t-to Paul Stack. You'll need to ask for a shell for an old NHC Blend. Check the date first. If you're asking on an odd numbered day, say *some things probably can't be fixed, but it's worth a shot if it's cheap enough*. If it's even numbered day, say *I cracked the edges and it spread around the back*. The wording is important; it'll tell him *I* sent you. Get it right and he'll set you up."

There's a moment of silence, and then Angel says, "Okay. We'll retrieve the stick, and if it looks like you're on to something, I'll make the necessary arrangements for payment. Cassie, finish up what you're doing, and head out there. There's no time like the present, after all. Once you have the stuff, check it over. I'd like to know what you think before we decide on the next steps. Oh, and take your time with it. I'll tell you where we can meet tomorrow."

And with that, the communicator goes dead. So, I head back to the bathroom, remove the earpiece and transmitter, and store them in a little box in the cupboard under the sink. "You say jump, I say how high," I mutter.

*

I wasn't aware the wishing well in the park existed until late last year when I stumbled across it by accident. I was angry with how a case was going and essentially stormed into the little clearing at the back of the wooded area without thinking. It's interesting because it looks like a traditional wishing well but isn't built like one. The part sticking out of the ground is a mix of traditional brick and plastic built to look like wood. If you look inside, you'll see the entire interior is a concrete tube rather than continued brickwork like you'd see in an actual old well.

It doesn't take long to find the loose brick Gary mentioned. Once I slide it out of place, I start digging with my hand entirely because I don't tend to carry small shovels with me. Luckily, while deep enough to be fully submerged in dirt, the little box isn't so far down as to be a problem. I remove the stick and phone from the box, replace it, and push the dirt back on top and then slide the brick back into place. Once I'm back in the car, I try switching the phone on, but it doesn't respond to either my button presses or my attempt to charge it. Removing the battery reveals why; the motherboard is not only visible but clearly water damaged.

Resigned to needing to do a little extra work, I make my way to T.J. Crest Repairs. The store is unremarkable to look at. It's small by modern standards, and the outside looks clean enough, but lacks the branding bigger chains have. That makes sense given who sent me here.

Inside, I can only see one staff member, a tall, tired-looking man sitting behind the counter. I walk over, and he raises an eyebrow at me. I nod back and say, "Hi. I'm looking for Paul Stack. Does he work here?"

The man sighs and drums his fingers on the counter. "You found him."

"Right. I'm kinda looking for something specific and was told you might be the guy to speak to."

"So says a lot of people. You an undercover cop?"

"No, just a customer."

"Uh-huh. Well let me make this clear. I don't do dodgy shit. You want stolen goods look elsewhere."

Sounds like someone's been having some trouble. Ignore the attitude and play nice. "No, no, nothing like that. Look, it's just—nowhere seems to stock what I'm after anymore, and a friend told me you may be a *Locke* to get it fixed."

He blinks, the emphasis on Gary's surname apparently registering the way I wanted, and asks, "What are you after?"

"I need a shell for an old NHC Blend," I say and think to the date. It's the twenty-second, so I continue, "I cracked the edges, and it spread to the back."

"You got the handset?"

I pull the broken one out of my pocket, and he looks it over. "Looks about right." He places it on the table and asks, "Is everything backed up?"

"Yeah, I got it all on a micro-USB."

"Okay, good. These things are rarely beyond repair, but they don't fix easily. Best option is I give you a replacement handset."

"How much?"

He shrugs. "I can always use a Blend. Straight trade is fine."

"Sounds good." An idea hits me, but I have to be careful. I look up and notice something is missing from the walls. "I just realised; you don't have any cameras up."

"Best not to, right?"

I nod. "Obviously, but I mean, what about security?"

Paul nods over my shoulder, and I turn to see a large man polishing a shotgun in the back corner of the store. I can't believe I missed him on the way in. I guess dark clothes and dark corners go a long way together. Still, the main thing is, there's no way for *anyone* to see what I'm about to do.

"More effective than a video clip of an intruder, eh? Anyway, sorry to be a pain, but could I take two phones?"

He narrows his eyes. "Why?"

"Well, from what I hear, my *friend* has been detained for a little while now, but he's going to be coming out my way soon. He has a fondness for the handset, so I thought it would be a nice surprise for him."

"That right?" Paul says, rubbing his chin. "Well then, I don't see why not. If he likes Blends, he's a man of taste, at least. I tell you what. I'll give you two, but you tell him not to be a stranger if he needs anything. Sound fair?"

"Absolutely."

Paul reaches under the counter and pulls out a lockbox. He opens it up and hands me two handsets. I give my thanks and slip them into my pocket before heading back to the car. So I don't look too suspicious, I drive away from the store and make my way to my apartment. Sitting on my comfy couch, I can relax enough to have a proper look at the phone.

The NHC Blend was the first to be manufactured in the city and had the sort of thinking behind it you'd expect; making use of a micro-USB slot for data transfer, New Hopeland branded parts, that sort of thing. If anything, the only surprise about its release was it took nearly fifteen years for a telecommunications company to move in.

This particular handset *is* interesting though. It's lighter than it should be, which the inbuilt diagnostics confirms is due to the speaker, camera, antennas, and Wi-Fi adapter all being missing. Scrolling through the app list, I realise it only has a few basic office things installed. For all intents and purposes, it's a file reader masquerading as a phone.

"I guess that's what he meant by not being connected to the New Hopeland network. This doesn't have the ability to connect to anything."

I pull the memory stick out of my pocket and plug it in, and the phone immediately starts copying the files across. It runs surprisingly quickly for such a basic piece of equipment and lets me know it's done within a few seconds. *Now for the tricky part.*

I lift the phone and intentionally drop it, being careful to catch it on my feet rather than let it hit the floor and risk breaking. "*Diu.*"

I lean over and nudge the phone onto the floor, carefully removing the memory stick as I do so. When I sit back up, I use my free hand to remove the second handset from my other pocket and switch it on while I lift it up. I plug the memory stick in and place the phone on the coffee table, making it look like it's taking its time. Carefully avoiding the other handset on the floor, I stand up, head to the kitchen, brew a coffee, and then come back. With the files already copied, I remove the stick, take a mouthful of liquid energy, and start reading a file named "Clean Up List."

The file appears to be a collection of profiles on people who have lived in the city over the years. A few of the names and faces look familiar, but I can't place them. The main thing of note is each and every person on the list has a criminal record.

The sixth profile I come to makes me pause.

I know the name listed as an alias.

I know the face.

I worked on their case way back when I first came to New Hopeland.

The case gave me far too many sleepless nights.

I stare at the photo on the screen, the same photo the PD gave me, and say, "You were my first TS Murder File."

The words on the screen start to sink in, and I realise, if this is all true, and then Gary Locke and his band of conspiracy theorists may not have been the bad guys after all.

Chapter Two

After a full evening looking through the files on the small screen, my head is spinning. I can see why Gary said not to review them on anything connected to the New Hopeland network because if everything is as closely monitored as Angel has hinted at, they'd definitely flag someone. I just wish he'd pointed me towards a full-size tablet. So, I treat myself to a normal person bedtime. And yes, when your workdays usually end closer to the next day, it *does* count as a treat.

Sleep comes surprisingly easy, as does waking up and resuming my trawl through the various theories. Finally, I message Angel, and she gives me an address to meet her at.

*

New Hopeland's Mall never ceases to amaze me. Most of the time, I find it hard to look at it as anything more than a mass of overpriced shops and oversnobbish citizens. Every once in a while, I find something there that surprises me. Previously, those surprises included a sewer entrance and a secret meeting space for video-chatting with the Four Kings of Utah. Today, it's The Last Clown, a strangely named, seedy-looking bar buried away at the back corner of the second floor.

To be fair, the inside doesn't appear entirely different to some of the bars I've visited to meet with the city's unsavoury types before. It's just a little darker and dirtier. So much so that, if it weren't for the sign reading "no purchase, no staying", I wouldn't have bought a drink at all. Unfortunately, I spotted Angel at the back of the room the moment I walked in, so there's no option to wait outside now. So, I buy the cheapest thing they're serving—something the bartender claims to be unbranded beer—and head over to Angel's booth. I slide into the seat opposite her and nod to her own glass. "Count yourself lucky you don't need to drink."

She smiles. "Technically, you don't need to either in this case. Once you've bought something, you can stay until it's gone if you want. I really wouldn't recommend drinking it, anyway. I've been watching them cleaning glasses behind the bar. Spit counts as soap here, it seems."

I wrinkle my nose at the thought and push the glass a little further away from myself. "Why this place? Why not stick at the warehouse?"

"I'm in a difficult position. If I stay in one place too long, I'm more likely to be caught due to prolonged activity. At the same time, I can't go just anywhere in the city, not since you tried to have me killed. Twice now you've almost ended my fun, isn't it?"

"I wasn't counting."

Angel laughs. "Anyway, the usual criminal haunts in the city are out, for obvious reasons. The Mall has enough entrances and people that I can blend in, and The Last Clown? Well, the patrons here aren't criminals, they're just shitty people. They value their privacy, though, so we can talk without worry, as long as we aren't *too* loud."

"Not criminals, so no links to the Kings. Is that what you're thinking?"

"Not necessarily, but it's more likely they don't have a direct link, simply because they have less to gain from it. Now, did you finish reading Gary Locke's files?"

I take an NHC Blend out of my pocket, along with the memory stick, and slide them across the table to Angel. "I did."

"And?"

"He certainly feels the same way you do as far as monitoring goes. There are plenty of notes about how all systems linked to the New Hopeland network are recorded and stored. Most of what's on here is personnel files. Profiles on various people who have come and gone in New Hopeland. He's been pretty thorough."

"Thorough in what way?"

"It looks like he's been keeping tabs on people who left the city with their life intact, at least if they were involved in any way with the government. That includes people who worked directly with the staff, people who had contracts of any size, and those who worked with officials via other people."

"Do they prove what he said about additional technology being built into public release items?"

I shrug. "I don't have a clue. There are a lot of things being bought and sold, but I'm not an engineer."

"Fair enough. You seem tense. There's something else, isn't there?"

"Yeah. Are you aware of the TS Murder Files?"

"Of course. What about them?"

"They got too rough for the PD to handle alone. When I first came to New Hopeland, those cases were my first collaborative effort with them. Locke had a file on one of the victims I investigated. Roger Watson. He was a freelance tech guy, no immediate family, and not enough remains for a funeral by the time we got there."

"Okay, so why did Locke have a file on him?"

"*If* what he found out is accurate, Roger Watson was an alias for a man named Leonard Tomes. He was a cop killer, tried and convicted three years prior. Thanks to a combination of his lawyer not being fond of the police and the boys in blue not exactly following protocol when they arrested him, his conviction was overturned. They gave him a new identity and sent him here. According to Locke's files, almost all the victims have a similar story. On top of that, each of the lawyers involved in the cases is bankrolled by one the Four Kings of Utah."

"So Casille brought them in."

"*If* this is all true."

"You don't seem certain, detective."

"I'm not. I don't trust Gary Locke."

She nods. "Understandable. Still, I'll review the files myself and see if anything seems out of place. It may all come down to finding out where he got his information from."

"I thought the same. So, why not pump the other former members of The Roots of Eden are Rotten for information first?"

"That's not an option, I'm afraid. Remember Frank Tyson?"

"Sure. NHPD's latest upstart tried to pin his death on me."

"Clearly you must have one of those faces," she says and flashes me a sideways grin. "Anyway, I tried it with him before, during, and after the torture. It turns out Locke tended to keep a lot of things to himself, at the very least while he classed them as a work in progress. Everything he gathered from the escapade with Dean Hollister and Eddie Redwood was raw data to him. He wouldn't tell anyone else involved what this whole scheme amounted to until he finished compiling it. If Frank hadn't decided to make himself part of the evidence against Locke, I suspect he would have turned this stick over to one of the other blog contributors to continue working on."

"Great. So, to get to the bottom of it all, the choices are work with Locke or do the work ourselves with no idea where to gather the rest of the information?"

"Yup. According to what he told Harold, there's more info he can provide. Once he's out, of course."

I sigh. "You're actually going to spring him, aren't you? Him and Harold Sanderson."

"No, *we're* going to spring Locke. Harold is staying inside. He's more useful there. For now."

"We, huh. You know I'm likely to kill him, eh?"

"You won't. Even without your clear curiosity about what's going on in the city, you aren't the type to kill without being able to justify it. And deep down, I think you know your issues with him, understandable as they are, aren't justification enough. You would have shot him the night he tried to kill you and your girlfriend if it was."

"*Diu lei.*"

"Temper. You know I'm right; both on your ability to kill in this instance and that we need him."

Calm down, Cassie. Think of it as a necessary evil. I take a deep breath, exhale, and stand up. "Fine. Call me when you have a plan."

I walk away and leave Angel to her plotting.

*

Knock-knock.

"Caw."

I watch Bert climb onto my worktable and position himself facing the front door. I rub his head and say quietly, "If she tries to kill me, take her down. Otherwise, stand down for now. I need to stay close to her."

"Caw."

"I'm always careful." Bert closes the rings around his eyes to narrow them at me, and I smile. "Yeah, I didn't think you'd buy that."

I open the door and let Angel in. She's carrying a large bag on her back. "This is the first time I've been here at the same time as you."

"I prefer it this way," I reply. "At least I know what you're doing if I'm here to watch."

She nods. "Hi, Bert."

Bert chatters his beak in response, making an angry *clack-clack-clack-clack* sound.

"The power's still on. The last time you met me here you switched everything off and used a hologram. Aren't you worried the security camera is recording you?"

Angel casually points her thumb over her shoulder at the camera and starts making herself at home. "I hacked it. It's currently showing a couple of loops of you from different times. It'll get picked up eventually if someone looks closely, but using a couple of compatible clips means I can have it vary enough not to be too obvious. I did the same with the hallways and the elevator. They cut to clear halls the moment I walked in."

"Good to know. So, I take it you have a plan to get Locke out?"

"That's right. We're going to be travelling to the prison in my current car; me in the front and you in the trunk."

"Stop. Why the trunk?"

"Because the security checkpoints take it all very seriously come the evening. There's a good chance at least one of them will know you. Me? I've got some fake ID and an equally fake meeting set up to discuss tech maintenance. Once we get there, you're going to retrieve Locke and bring him out front."

"So, you're worried the security checkpoints will recognise me but not the staff I've interacted with countless times? And why do I have to be the one to do the breakout?"

"You should trust me more, Cassie. First of all, you need to do the breakout because *you* are more expendable than me. If this all goes wrong, I'll need a second shot at it. That becomes much harder if it's me who gets caught. Second of all, they won't recognise you unless they apprehend you, because you'll be wearing this."

She throws me the bag, and I catch it. I unzip the top and look inside. "An LV suit?"

"That's right. Modified for this purpose. The body armour is heavier than the ones Harold and I wore because you live and learn, right? The helmet will allow you regular vision rather than the standard display with heart monitors and so on."

"No. I don't like this."

"I also have this," she says, pulling a small disc out of her pocket. "To shut down Bert there if I need to. You see, Cassie, I *want* us to be able to work together on this on as close to equal terms as I can allow. However, you know enough that if you try to back out or tell anyone what I'm doing, then I will have no choice but to kill you. That would be such a waste, especially as I'm taking a lot of steps to ensure you stay alive through tonight's festivities."

"Yeah? Like what?"

"Let's just say I have *a lot* of tools at my disposal. Now, unless you really want to end things here, I suggest you go and get changed. There's a long coat in the bag to hide the main suit, and I suggest you leave the helmet in the bag until you're in the trunk. Oh, and when you free Locke, don't mention Casille or his link to the Kings. We need him to keep digging, but I only want him playing in the holes he's already started."

I sigh and grab the bag. "Fine."

*

The hard bumping under my body lets me know Angel has taken us off road. Once we stop moving, the engine noise drops to a low murmur. *She's keeping the engine running. Which means she expects us to need to make a quick escape. Great.*

The lock on the trunk clicks and opens. It's dark out, so I don't have to worry about much in the way of temporary blindness. Angel offers me a hand and I take it, letting her pull me up to my feet. "You were right," I say. "It takes a little while to get used to breathing in the helmet."

"That's why I said to put it on while you're in there," she replies, her voice crystal clear in the helmet speaker. "It gives you the chance to acclimatise to it."

I nod. "It feels odd. Restrictive."

"But workable?"

"Yeah. So how is this going to work?"

"Simple." She turns and I follow her gaze. We're standing behind a rock a short way from the outside of the prison, hidden behind the solid mass and the dip below us. "It's dark enough that your suit will provide some camouflage. So, as long as you move quietly, you'll make it to the wall without issue. From there, I'll be able to guide you."

"How?"

"I have access to the live feed on the cameras, same as the designated guard for the evening."

"Eyes everywhere, eh."

"Exactly that."

"Then why not hack them like you've been doing with mine at home? Wouldn't that make the break-in—and out—easier?"

She shakes her head. "I could cut them, but that would alert him. Stock footage would be too difficult in this case too; the guards rotate who is patrolling where regularly, and the guy with the camera feed has a list of who to expect, when, and where. Without footage of the right person in the right area with the right lighting conditions, he'd know. Short bursts will work, but I can't set up a long-term loop."

"That's going to make it difficult."

"Yup. That's why you're gonna need to kill him."

I pale, and my muscles tense, but I know what I need to say. "No."

"Hmm?"

Angel tilts her head towards me, and I shake my head to reiterate the point. "No. I'm not killing anyone. Not here."

"Really? You do want to get to the bottom of things, don't you?"

"I do, but I draw the line on killing innocents. I'm not Harold Sanderson. I won't be your attack dog."

She shrugs. "You always did strike me as the sort who likes to make things difficult for themselves. Fine. I tell you what. I want us to be able to trust each other. So, I'll trust your judgement, and make you a promise: I will not intentionally kill anyone myself tonight unless it becomes an absolute necessity."

"Including me?"

"Especially you. Like I said, I've been taking steps to ensure you stay alive. With luck, none of my contingencies will be needed. Just be aware the longer you take, the more likely you are to get caught."

"I know. Okay. Let's get this over with."

Angel adjusts her headset slightly and moves to the front seat of the car, where she opens a laptop. She regards the screen for a moment and then says, "You should be safe. If you don't want to kill the watcher at the front, and then you'll need to head to...the right-hand corner of the wall directly in front of us. Move quickly, and I'll give you further instructions from there."

I do as I'm told, climbing carefully out from behind our hiding place, and jogging towards the wall, keeping my body low. Once I'm there, I straighten up and push my back to it. Angel's voice says, "There are no cameras on that side, but there is a guard. Check, slowly."

Like a good little doggy, I obey the command, sliding to my left and slowly leaning my head around the corner. The guard on patrol is walking away from me. Even though the helmet is soundproof, I naturally drop into a whisper when I say, "You getting this?"

"Yes. The camera on the helmet is pretty good, so don't worry too much. Once he rounds the corner, he'll be walking right towards a camera. I can track him again from there. And there he goes. Start following his path. There should be a door somewhere around there."

I keep walking, taking care to move as near to silently as I can, and study the wall as I go. "No doors yet, and I doubt going over the top is going to work. It's way too high for me to climb, and I didn't see any of the jumping booster things on the boots for this suit."

"No, they take far too long to get used to using. Edge to the corner and wait. The door is on the next wall." She pauses and the next few seconds seem like an eternity. "Okay. The guard is out of camera shot. I've taken three seconds of clear footage and started it looping. With the regularity of the patrols, you should have a little over a minute to get by the camera. After that, I'll need to switch it back to the live feed. I suggest you move, now."

Without pausing, I step around the corner and start jogging. I can see the camera pointing towards me and can't help but breathe a sigh of relief once I've passed it. Just beyond it, I come to a door. A quick press of the handle confirms what I expected. "Locked."

I feel a small vibration on my left thigh and look down. One of the thick panels has slid aside, revealing a small box.

"Put that on the lock."

"What is it?"

"The thing that will get you caught if you insist on an explanation."

"Point taken." I place the box on the lock, and it immediately magnetises itself. I hear a hiss, and after a few seconds, it slips off. Looking closer, I realise what happened. The box has melted part of the lock away.

"Take the box with you," Angel instructs as I open the door and sneak in. "You can drop it anywhere in there, there's no camera. Pull the door shut behind you too."

"Won't the next guard notice the melted lock?"

"Not sure. The guard didn't check it on the way back from what I could see. Whether he did on the way through, I don't know. Best keep moving. Looking at the plans, you're close to one of the staff fire exit corridors. It's not on the list of places that are being watched, so I'll put a short loop in on the cameras. There. Head through the door, follow it around to the end, and wait there."

The corridor is longer than I expected and clearly runs the entire length of the eastern wall of the complex. Just as I've been told, I reach the end and wait. "Okay, now whe—"

The door to my left clicks, cutting me off, and a voice starts grumbling its way out. "Damn clogged toilets making me head all the way here."

"*Diu.*"

The guard steps out from what I'm now assuming is a staff toilet and starts to turn in my direction. Before I can even think of a plan, my body reacts; I slam my right fist into the side of his head, causing him to fall unconscious to the floor. I didn't mean to do that. I didn't want to do that. It was as if something pulled my body into place. *Or someone.* "What did you do?"

"Those suits are like flesh bags, in a way. And I can control a flesh bag from the other end of the country if I have to. I told you, Cassie. I have contingencies in place to keep you alive. *This* means a variable has been introduced, and the main plan has changed. I'll keep my promise, but I'm taking over."

Before I can respond, my body jerks into action again and throws the door open. There's a strange disconnect as I speed through the hallways, effortlessly tackling guards as I go. The sound of the alarm invades my head, and I start to panic. My body stops at a cell door, and something vibrates on my right thigh. I can't even turn my head to look, but I know the feel of the item when my hand grabs it. A gun. My hand pulls the trigger, firing three shots into the lock, and I barge it open.

Gary Locke is pushed into the back corner of the room. He looks at me as my left arm shoots up and beckons him to follow. We step out of the door and another guard charges around the corner. To my horror, my right hand—and the gun—rise into view, and two bullets are sent into her. "Shoulder and leg," Angel says over the speakers. "She'll live."

As we run by, the guard tries to raise her gun, and my foot shoots out, hitting her hand with more force than I'd like.

"Two corridors to go. You're about to be back in the saddle, Cassie. Don't panic when you reach the front door."

The release of pressure on my body is instantly noticeable, but as if they've been conditioned, my legs keep running. Desperation to finish this job is setting in. When we hit the final corridor, my hope for a quick resolution starts to fade away. There are three more guards blocking the exit, each with guns trained on us. Locke ducks behind me, and one of the guards steps forward. "Stay where you are and slowly lower your gun to the ground. If you try to run, one of us will shoot you. If you shoot, one of us will shoot you."

I flip the gun so I'm holding the barrel and start to drop to one knee, but something slams against the glass door we were heading towards, drawing all three guards' attention. One yells, "Oh, shit," and they all dive to the side, barely avoiding the flying glass as the little metal box explodes, shattering the door inward.

"Cover your eyes," Angel's voice says, and I turn around and bring one hand up. Something else explodes, showering the hallway in light. "Now, quickly."

I grab Gary Locke by the shoulder and, realising he was caught with the flashbang, drag him forward towards the exit. We run and don't stop until we're back at the car. I throw Gary into the front passenger seat, dive into the back, and try to remove my helmet while Angel speeds us away from the building.

"See? No deaths," Angel says.

"What about the security checkpoints?"

"Have a look to your right."

I sit up. Angel is taking us off-road. In the dark of the night, I spot the headlights of a car power on. The vehicle drives onto the road and speeds towards the security checkpoints I'd mentioned. "Who is that?"

"A couple of associates. They're in LV suits, their licence plates match these, and they have a passenger who'll pass for Mister Locke here in the dark. Don't worry, I have faith they'll make it through, but if not, then the idea is for the fake passenger to flee. If that fails, too, we'll be long gone by then. Of course, they'll get the PD to keep an eye out for LVs, so I'm gonna need you to get changed."

"Here?"

"No, we'll find somewhere. No need to give our colleague here a strip show."

*

Angel kept her word. We found an abandoned building to park behind, and she kept Locke distracted with I'm assuming talk about his theories while I changed behind some boxes. If I'm being honest, I did smile when she instructed *him* to climb into the trunk in order to stay hidden. By the time she's dropped me a few blocks from home, I've calmed down a bit. And so, my walk through the lobby, to the elevator, and up the hallway to my front door is relatively quiet.

When I step back in, Bert immediately greets me. "I'm fine," I say and give his head a rub, being careful to let my finger match the pattern I traced before I opened the door to Angel. That's one of the perks of Bert's model; he has a sensor just below the back of his head that works like a touchpad on a laptop. Angel said she'd take care of making sure my security camera footage synchs up again, so I take myself straight to the bathroom and stand in front of the mirror.

"Why couldn't the one room that isn't monitored be the one with the comfy couch in it? Okay, Cassie, think. Bert recorded the conversation with Angel, which means we have proof she threatened you. It's only on internal storage right now, so we can get that on the spare Blend. If I wasn't certain she was still monitoring the mini communicator, I could have worn that and caught the stuff she said during the breakout too." I sigh. "No sense in worrying about the things you didn't do. Just keep moving forward. Keep seeing this through until you have a clear path to follow."

I nod to my reflection, happy for the advice, and head back to the kitchen to make a drink.

Chapter Three

"Long night?" I ask, nodding toward Gary Locke, who appears to be slumped in an elderly computer chair, snoring less than softly.

"He was quite eager to start recovering his old files, so I gave him the tools to do so," Angel replies. "It's all automated from here, apparently, so he's catching up on what sleep he missed out on last night. And what about you? Was the rest of the night more restful for you after we parted ways?"

I pull another of the loose chairs out and sit in it, staring directly at Angel. "Not really, no. Violence against innocents tends to leave me on edge. Especially when I'm forced into it."

Angel laughs and spins her own chair from side to side. "*This*, all of this, Cassie, is simply me doing what I need to to survive. Most people do that and usually in the only way they know how. Take yourself for example. What is the main goal you have for each case you take on?"

"It depends on the case."

She rolls her eyes and continues, "All right then, let me rephrase it. At their core, what do all your cases have in common once they're done?"

I sigh. "I get paid, which is how I pay my bills, and so survive."

"Exactly. Now, most of the people you find yourself in opposition to are objectively bad people, I'm sure. Whether it be infidelity or a direct threat to someone else's life, they've all committed crimes, be they legal or moral. Of course, some of them do what they do by choice, I'm sure. You don't have to jump into bed with the first person to show you attention, and so on. How many of them, though, are simply trying to eke out a living? Their methods may not always be savoury, but for a lot of criminals, their crimes are their jobs. It's how they provide for themselves and their families. Perhaps they made some bad choices to end up that way, or perhaps they just couldn't see another option. Either way, is what they're doing *really* so different to what you do?"

"It's completely different."

"Is it? A mugger intimidates a victim, you intimidate a mugger. A low-end drug dealer shoots a client who owes them money; you shoot a dealer who threatens your client. A killer mutilates their victim; you set Bert on them. Same method, different angle. And let's not forget the company you keep, Cassie. Can you really say people like Devin Carmichael and Charlotte Goldman are good people? They may have their own moral codes, but when it comes to it, they're still a cold-blooded killer and a drug lord."

I shake my head. "That's the thing. Their moral code sets them apart. It's what stops them being nothing more than their jobs."

"You see, I don't think it does. You add too many shades of grey, and you stop seeing the picture beneath it. You should try simplifying your world view; it's very freeing. Ah, but that isn't possible for you, is it? What was it Ethan Cobalt said to you? *You are in the unique position whereby you stand equally in both light and dark, and do not attempt to hide this.* That's part of your persona, isn't it? You can't help but see the grey, at least when it suits you."

I narrow my eyes. I can ignore the jab at my apparently inconsistent approach to people, but what she said beforehand bothers me. "He said that back before I caught Malcolm Castleford. How long have you been monitoring everything?"

Angel's lips curl into a satisfied smile, and she leans forward in her chair. She waves a finger at me and says, "That's much better. Right question, Cassie. Simple answer. Not as long as you're now thinking."

"Then how did you know what he said to me on a private call?"

"I know because I took something from you back when we first met."

I involuntarily shiver at the thought of our first confrontation and fix her with a glare. "My blood."

"Exactly. It's amazing what you can do with someone's blood in this city. Can you guess how?"

"Cut this dancing around things, Angel. You want me to trust you and work with you, but you won't tell me anything."

"Oh, come now. The esteemed Mister Locke over there figured it out, and I know you wouldn't want to be outdone by *him*, right?"

"This is ridiculous," I growl, my frustration bubbling over. "Right now, I couldn't care less about whether Gary Locke figured out something I didn't. My career puts me up against people who know stuff I don't all the time. I still expect the people I'm working with to tell me what I need to know because otherwise, it gets dangerous for all of us. If you won't explain things to me, I could easily screw up, and that risks both our lives. It's reckless."

"I didn't get to where I am by being reckless, Cassie. Even the more brazen steps I've taken over the years have had purpose, and that includes everything I'm doing here. I *will* tell you, of course, but you're forgetting something. I've been watching you. And those around you. You're like a cute little bunny. You love to dig. And when you find something, you love to chew on it."

Angel pauses and clicks her tongue. After a moment, she nods, seemingly deciding on something, and continues. "Okay, the point on trust was fair. So, I'll be honest with you. In part, I'm not telling you yet because I want to keep you interested. There's also a touch of curiosity though; I want to see if you *can* figure it out. It was easy for Gary there because of the methods he uses, and his willingness to accept things that seem ridiculous. But you work with logic and old school investigating. I want to know if two roads can lead to the same place. Mostly, I want to keep you distracted."

"Distracted from what?"

"Your natural urges. You really are interested in what's happening in New Hopeland, but maintaining the status quo is also important to you. Giving you little tasks like this, even if it's a duplication of work, keeps you from running straight for the side you tend to stick with."

My mouth hangs open in shock, and it takes me a moment to compose myself. "Won't telling me that make your approach less effective?"

She shrugs. "I doubt it. I've paid attention, and I feel like I know you well enough to make a judgement call here. I think you'll do what I want because you simply don't have enough knowledge yet to be close to confirming the truth. You know what's implied, though, and it doesn't sit right with you."

On that point, she has you. You don't have a choice, Cassie; you're going to have to keep playing her game for now. Just be careful not to go so far you can't turn back. I shake the thoughts away and stand up. "Fine. But I want confirmation if I get something right."

"That sounds reasonable. Once Locke has finished transferring his files, we'll move forward again. Until then, go ahead and chew over what you know so far. Even the things you don't trust yet. Enjoy yourself. It'll help with the harder times to come."

*

"Here you go, Caz, your hazelnut thing," the waitress says, placing a steaming mug of latte down on the table in front of me.

"Thank you," I reply and turn the handle to face me.

"No Lori today," the waitress notes. "You must be working a case."

I smile and glance up at her. "What makes you say that?"

"Well, we do well enough here, but Cartwright's isn't exactly the Mall in terms of through traffic, is it? You have to do something to pass the time. Personally, I like to pay attention to the regulars. Spot the patterns and so on."

I laugh and cross my arms. "Well, at least I'm not the only spy in the room. So, what did you learn about me?"

"That you tend to come in for two reasons. One, if you're on a date with Lori."

"They're not all dates," I cut in. "Sometimes, we just happen to have time free at the same time and want to grab a decent coffee."

She shrugs. "Close enough to a date to count. And two, when you've got an investigation on and need to think. I can tell when that's the case pretty easily now."

"Oh? And how's that?"

"Because Lori's not here, and you aren't looking out the window every couple of seconds like a little lost dog. Enjoy the latte."

I smile and wave her on. Ordinarily, I'd be upset about someone spying on me, but the staff here are pleasant enough for it not to bother me. Plus, even if Cartwright's wasn't the best coffee shop in the city, it's not like she picked up on anything problematic. Still, I'm gonna be way more self-conscious when I'm waiting for Lori now.

Okay, back to work.

I sip at my drink and try to gather my thoughts a little.

What do I know for certain?

Nothing. That's why I hate this. It's like a partially completed puzzle, but the box doesn't tell you what it's meant to look like, and half the pieces are face down.

I drown the negativity in another dangerously large gulp of caffeine and shake my head.

Let's rework the question. What do I know we're considering? Government monitoring, blood samples, and government contracts.

Angel is definitely monitoring a lot of stuff, so there must be some truth to the concept of a main network. And she claims she's seen older files, too, which makes it likely that some things *at least are being stored.*

Since the method appears to be working, I take another sip of nut-flavoured brain juice.

The contract details looked pretty legitimate, but without seeing exactly what Locke dug up, I can't say it's definitely accurate. I can't review the second Blend here, and he hasn't finished recovering the rest of the files yet. So that leaves the blood. What do I know about blood?

Flashes of my high school biology class run through my head. It makes about as much sense now as it did then. I like science, and I have a basic understanding of a bunch of stuff, but it wasn't my strongest subject. Some of it did come up again during my time in the Academy back in Vancouver though.

Blood contains red and white blood cells. White cells contain DNA. Forensics teams use DNA to place someone in a specific place during a specific time. The results are used to strengthen or weaken a case. Were any of the contracts for things that could sample DNA?

I roll my eyes at the thought and take another drink.

How would you know that, eh? It's not like any of them said super-secret DNA reader or anything. But could it be used with the monitoring?

I'm about to kick myself again but a smile creeps onto my face instead.

If the government really is monitoring everything, regular people wouldn't like it too much. So, how would they pass it off as necessary? It'd be officially categorised as a security initiative. I may not know how the technical stuff works, but we've got plenty of home security firms here, and they all have shop floors with people working on commission.

Yeah. Let's run with that. First, though, I'm finishing this coffee.

*

The New Hopeland Mall is where people want to go when they want to feel rich. The clothing stores are high-end and fashion-forward, and the food is priced like it's being served in a five-star restaurant. If I ever lose what little sense I have left, I may stop by there to try out a five-dollar doughnut at a caviar price. The electronic shops are more varied. It's all decent stuff, but it's not what you'd see in most professional situations. With the odd exception, it mostly fits into the category of electronics people buy when they want to *appear* rich. I like to think of them as status symbol circuit boards. What that means is they contain the up-to-date popular features, but not necessarily the really useful stuff.

It's for that reason I avoided the two security stores there and instead headed to the large building I'm now realising is unsurprisingly close to Allen Fuerza's usual base of operations. It's one of those buildings you can tell used to be a warehouse by the shape of it. You can also tell it's not anymore by the simple-but-huge sign hanging above the door reading "Home Security: All Budgets Store."

Inside, I start following the trail of prices, avoiding the cheap equipment and heading more towards the newer, more costly items.

Looking at the tech specs on the labels, I'm beginning to wish Joe Farrah was an option. Even if Angel was wrong, he'd know the answers to what I need to find out. These guys don't tend to explain things too well unless motivated either, which means I'm gonna need to be sneaky. *Okay, let's try to look interesting.*

I pick up a box for some sort of camera and pretend to read the details on the back, making sure I'm in full sight of the store's cameras. I make a show of scratching my chin and then replace the box and move on to the security locks and repeat the process. After a couple of minutes, a wary-looking shop assistant walks up beside me. He crosses his arms and stares without saying a word, so I smile sweetly, put the box back, and pick up another one. The man finally clears his throat and comments, "You don't look like you can afford this stuff."

I stop what I'm doing and shake my head. "On my own, no. That's fine, because my own needs are fairly simple." I turn to face him and continue, "My client though? That's a different story."

I offer him my hand and he shakes it, though he's still clearly uncertain about me. I push on. "Caroline Tam. I'm a consultant out in Hooper."

"Hooper, huh? They've got some good stores in Hooper. So why come here?"

"My client is looking to beef up his security systems. The thing is, he doesn't really understand the tech, but he has friends who do. You're right that the selection is good there, but he'd be able to verify the pricing and uses far too easily. That makes it a hard sell for me."

"Simon Jones," he says relaxing a little now. He must have met people like the one I'm playing before. And regularly too. "You'll be wanting the New Hopeland exclusive kits then. What sort of thing is he looking for?"

"Mostly monitoring stuff. But I reckon I can convince him a few other things are a necessity, too, *if* I can get him everything he wants from one outlet. You work on commission, right?"

"Of course, for large orders."

"I'm already getting ten per cent of the cost as a fee, so my plan was to take the dairy farm approach."

"Go big or get out."

"Exactly. I was thinking, I reckon I could find everything he needs here. We could throw in a couple of justifiable but not necessary additional pieces, some insurance, and maybe a six per cent price increase—we'll call it a tip but forget to list it separately on the bill—and that'd be job done. We both get our commission and split the six per cent fifty-fifty."

"Hmm. I won't get commission on the tip. So how about we raise it to seven per cent and split it seventy-thirty in my favour?"

"How about sixty-forty?"

"Done. Okay, what sort of thing are we looking at for the core order?"

"Well, any high-end camera set will work for him. If it looks expensive and has prestige attached to the brand, he'll be happy. The big thing will be the footage storage and access. He wants something that can be linked with the cameras but be foolproof in terms of who can access the system. Oh, and by the way, I'm gonna need to sell this all to him, so I'll need two things from you. One, an itemised proposed bill. And two, I'm gonna need you to explain the stuff to me in terms an average Joe could understand."

"He's not knowledgeable at all then?"

"That's part of it. There's also me. I understand enough to know when someone is lying, but I'm more of a money moving woman than a tech spec woman, eh?"

He nods. "Well, with access points, we have three options that go above the standard password or card system. Fingerprinting is the cheapest, so he won't be wanting that. Eye scanners are incredibly popular, and we do have top-of-the-line models, but if we're looking to push this into real money, we could look at bloodprinting."

Bingo. "Okay, what's bloodprinting?"

"It's a combination of fingerprint scanning and DNA testing. Basically, the scanner takes a copy of the fingerprint and a blood sample, and tests both."

"Do the DNA tests take long?"

"A couple of minutes in most cases, so it's definitely not a quick access thing. As far as outright security goes, though, it's the best there is. It's only just started going mainstream as a system, so to keep ahead of the curve, New Hopeland has its own upgrade. Basically, the scanner takes the sample itself, and is built to register whether the wound is pulsating or simply leaking. It's like a built-in heart monitor."

"Interesting. And why is that an upgrade?"

"Well, as an example, let's say someone is using this system to lock their safe. To open it, you'd need both the matching fingerprint and blood sample. Now, if we assume a burglar knows about the system, and the owner isn't the sort who will just give in and open it up, there aren't many options. Most likely, they'd kill the owner and remove a finger or the whole hand. The scanner will know if the finger is still attached to a living body, and if it's not, won't open it without an override."

"So, an old-fashioned code?"

He shakes his head again. "That's the joy of this system. The owner would store a sample of their blood at a bank or hospital, and it would be tainted with a specific nanochip. You place the vial in the core control box, and that'll open the system."

"And the nanochip would be unique to that particular setup?"

"Absolutely. And the scan would need both the chip and a specific amount of blood to be present for it to work."

"Fascinating. Will it only work with the system storage?"

"Nope, you could apply it to anything that needs locking. Of course, the timing issue remains there, so here's what I'd propose: we go full hybrid. The main system runs using New Hopeland bloodprinting, but we also install a retinal scanner. That way, he could open his computers, cameras, or even doors with his eyes if he's in a hurry, while still keeping everything secure. It means all his stuff would be harder to crack."

"And the cost would go way up to install it on everything."

He smiles. "We'd apply a discount, of course. Given the cost, it would make it more appealing without overly impacting our own profit."

"I like how this is sounding."

"Everything else we could throw in would be high-end but fairly standard in operation, so I tell you what. I'll show you some options, you can ask any questions you may have in order to sell it to your client, and we'll run some figures."

I wave my hand to beckon him to lead me on, and we start a quick run through the aisles.

*

I return to my car with a three-page price list, and the second I shut the door, my phone rings. It's Angel, so I answer. "You really are watching everything, aren't you?"

"Not all at once. Right now, I'm watching you. For a security firm, the audio on their in-store equipment isn't great. Still, I rather enjoyed the show. I like it when you lie. It amuses me."

"All part of the job."

"*That*, we have in common. So, what are your thoughts?"

"Wait...is this okay to talk about on the phone?"

"Don't worry. I'm the only one listening, and I fully intend to delete the audio file, the call log, and the automated manuscript once we're done. The government systems are wonderfully easy to work when you get used to them. I'm assuming they outsourced."

"Great. Now I'm thinking back to the dumb stuff I've said on the phone before."

"I wouldn't worry. Nobody cares how you choose to embarrass yourself unless you give them cause to. Remain careful, remain a footnote. Now, come on. What are you thinking?"

"I'm thinking...you and Sanderson hiding out in the hospital wasn't only because it gave you access to Pauline Welch."

"Go on."

"All new arrivals in the city are given a free medical check-up, which included the doctors taking a couple of blood samples. The regular check-ups include the same even if you're not looking at a specific potential illness. The samples are taken and stored to be used as access points, aren't they? In case someone needs to review part of someone's monitored life?"

"Well done, Cassie. Is that all you figured out?"

"No, there's more to it. Something the store guy said stuck with me."

"Which is?"

"Nanochips. You're still able to monitor me, even after your tracker was removed. I'm confident the checks the doctors did are correct, and you didn't leave anything else there. Which means the regular blood tests leave something small behind. Something *you* could access by taking blood. Given you took blood from the neck, it's something that moves. And there has to be more than one. I just don't know what *it* is."

"Yet. If you figure it out, I'll tell you you're right."

"Somehow, I thought you'd say that."

She pauses and then says, "You sound tired. You should go and visit Lori. You arranged to meet her tonight, right?"

I sigh because what else can I do about the intrusion into my private life? "Yeah. I did. I'll talk to you tomorrow."

I hang up and take a moment to calm myself and then head home to grab Bert.

*

"Well, I better start getting changed. He seems pretty relaxed."

I give Bert a pat on the head. "He does, doesn't he? I think you were right though; it's better we do this here. Too much stimuli gets him a little short tempered."

Lori nods. "We're all like that, I think. So, listen. Ink will probably seem a little different during this."

"Okay. Why's that?"

"Bert's familiar with *me*. I was planning not to go into my headspace for this. I figured I'd rather retain all the familiarity, just in case."

"That makes sense. I can still see you in there when you're Ink though."

She smiles and gives me a gentle kiss on the cheek. "That's because you've been around us enough now to take the two of us as one package."

"It *would* seem strange for you to be one and not the other."

"Didn't you think Tech Shifting itself was strange?"

"I did. I guess I still do, to a point. I mean, it's not something I have an urge to *do*, so understanding it fully is difficult, eh? What I do understand is it works for you. It's important to you, and it's a part of you. Knowing that makes it hard for me to picture living without it around me."

Lori giggles. "Apart from admitting you find Ink strange, that was pretty sweet. You're getting better at romantic stuff. Sort of."

I run a hand through my hair without thinking about it and reply, "I'm…trying to let my guard down quicker around you. I know you aren't out to get me, but I'm also aware that most of the rest of the city *is*."

Lori leans in close enough I can feel her breath on my ear when she whispers, "I don't need to be out to get you, I've already got you." She must hear my breath catch, and there's a smile in her voice as she stands up and says, "I'll give you a shout when I'm ready."

As she walks out of the room, I can't help but think, *And I have you.*

One of the things that surprises me the most with Lori is the teasing. In the past, if someone intentionally tried to get me embarrassed, I would have thrown them into the "get out of my life" pile. Literally, once.

That's because you were hurting. You liked it when you were with Charlie. And now, you like being with someone who knows you well enough to know exactly *how to get a reaction from you.*

I shake the voice away and turn my attention to Bert, who's busy investigating his favourite corner of Lori's couch. All things considered I need this tonight. At home, I have so many surveillance options because I'm naturally paranoid. Okay, it's all cameras and audio recording, and they're all cheap, but they work. That's the important thing. Ordinarily, glancing up and seeing a camera stems my own fear mongering but with all this stuff going on with Angel? They're making it worse. I'm second guessing what the government may have seen in the past and getting nervous Hoove will have to send someone to bust in and arrest me before I can figure out how to deal with it all.

Lori is the opposite of me. She has the bare minimum installed here. It's decent equipment, a couple of steps up from my most basic stuff, but there isn't much of it. Not feeling like I'm being watched is suddenly far more of a comfort than I ever thought it could be.

"Okay, I'm ready."

I get to my feet and look at Bert. "Wait."

"Caw."

Leaving the living room, I turn right and walk up the hallway to the door to Lori's bedroom. Honestly, it's surprising how spacious her bungalow is. From the outside, it looks pretty small, but as she pointed out to me when I mentioned it, it goes back a fair way. I reach the door and give it a nudge open, and Ink walks out. We'd agreed I should introduce her to Bert rather than have her just walk in. Watching her beside me, I realise Lori was right. There's a difference in Ink's walk. I can't even put my finger on what it is exactly, but it's definitely there. It's comfortable, well-practised, but less feline somehow.

"Bert," I say, as we go back into the living room. "This is Ink."

Bert ignores us, finding the company of a loose thread on the couch far more interesting.

I rub the bridge of my nose and sigh. Lori giggles from somewhere within Ink and makes her way over to him. She slowly raises a metallic paw and gives him a light rap on the head.

Bert stops what he's doing and opens his beak but stops short of saying anything when he sees the big black panther staring at him.

"Bert, this is Ink," I try again.

The rings around his eyes open and close a little as he looks Ink over. Finally, he says, "Caw."

Ink sits back, slowly beginning to look more catlike in motion now, and flicks her tail back and forth.

Bert regards Ink and then hops down from the couch and waddles over, watching the panther's tail move. After a few seconds, he makes a grab for it, but Ink flops it further to the side and stops still. When he moves towards her tail, she flops it back the other way again. Seeing how the game is going, Bert takes a step back and seems to think about his next move.

Ink watches.

I sit myself down onto the couch and do the same.

Bert steps forward and starts to scramble up Ink's body, but she lets herself fall to the side and rolls onto her back, paws up as she tilts her head towards the metal gargoyle that's falling less than elegantly off her side. Bert, undeterred, comes in again, and Ink rolls onto her front and starts pawing at the floor just in front of him. In a moment of pure mechanical athleticism, Bert leaps back. And crashes into my shin.

"Hey! Ow!"

Bert turns and looks at my shin and then angles his head up towards my face and gives me a stern, "Caw."

That was a "watch where you put your feet," I think. So, I pull my legs up onto the couch and rub the sore spot. "Thanks for the concern, Bert."

But it's too late, he's already trying to tag Ink's paws as she bounds around, now much more like herself.

*

"I am so sorry about your shin."

I pull my arm a little tighter, and Lori snuggles right into my shoulder, her free arm reaching across me to rest on my other shoulder. "Most people don't giggle when they're sorry."

"Defence mechanism," she says, stifling a yawn.

"You know, you were right. Ink seemed different at first. I could tell when you dropped into just being her though."

Lori nods. "It's hard not to when I'm in the gear. Still, I loved Bert's complete lack of surprise when I took her off in front of him."

"I think he must have known. He registers body heat and stuff like that, so maybe he saw who was inside and recognised the shape of you or something."

"I would have played with him longer, but he was so full-on. Especially compared to the meets."

"You all have human stamina, and he has robo-destroyer stamina."

Lori lets out a squeak that was probably a short laugh and shifts her head to look at where Bert has powered down to charge. "That's true. I still wouldn't be sure about him coming to a meet though. So many of us might get him overexcited, and I'm not sure all of them could keep up with him."

"Jane's husband, Murphy. He could. Have you seen how fast he runs after that ball? He's pretty non-stop all night when they're there."

"That's true. Maybe we could get them over for a double play date. We'll keep Bert amused, and you two can chat about how great I am."

I laugh. "Maybe. I like Jane. She's very straightforward when she talks to me. It's refreshing in my line of work."

"That's because, to the criminals, you're a big bully."

"Hey," I say, tilting her head to mine for a kiss. "The bad guys deserve it."

"Mmm. And what do I deserve?"

Two can play that game. I lean forward and lower my voice to a near purr. "Why don't we go to bed, and you can find out?"

Her hand on my shoulder tenses, and now it's her turn to have her breath catch. She raises her lips to my neck, and we don't quite make it to the door.

Chapter Four

The night with Lori helped a lot. It gave me a chance to calm down and rest, which has left me much more capable of wearing my normal work mask. It even makes Gary Locke's babbling bearable. Almost.

"...and so you see, the network is not entirely secure. But what is these days? The main thing, M-Miss Tanner, is there is enough security in place to ensure it is not easily hacked by anyone, even the government."

"What about the people online who spend their free time breaking stuff?" I ask.

"Like who?"

"There are plenty of websites hidden away on the net where people go to test viruses or try their hand at breaking security systems."

Locke smiles. "My systems are built b-by people like you mention. Unless they are pointed in this direction, they will have no reason to try getting through it all. And even then, it would be hard for them to find anything."

Angel, who has been listening quietly so far, asks, "And why is that?"

"Because, M-Miss Tanner, Eddie Redwood left behind a legacy of useful tools. These files move around automatically, migrating to different servers regularly. If one is breached, the system will pick up on it and instigate another move."

I sigh. "Is there really that much more for us to see?"

"Oh yes. There always was. Even *The Roots of Eden are Rotten* was merely a window into our research. Think of the blog like a movie trailer, teasing the audience with promises of what's to come."

"Trailers rarely give you an accurate depiction of what's coming," I reply.

"Quite so. We meant the blog as a way of enticing others to the cause. To get people talking, cause civil unrest, start the blind on the road to revolution."

"So you're a coward then."

"A coward?"

"Yeah. If you truly wanted to cause a revolution, you would have either published the full findings online or moved ahead with what you knew yourself. At best, you were hoping someone else would kick up enough of a storm for the hidden things to fall out."

"You misunderstood us, M-Miss Tam. We always intended to move ahead when the research was complete. On top of that, publishing everything would lead to the articles being buried and us along with it. Leaving a few blanks intrigues others enough to act. People naturally *want* to fill them in. Plus, you never reveal your full hand before it's time. That gives your enemies more time to find a counter."

"As much as I enjoy discussing the joys of criminal philosophy," Angel cuts in, "we are on a time limit here. And one where we don't actually know the limit. How many more files are left to transfer?"

"Oh, I am confident they're all done. I intended to check with the remaining members, just in case they had something new but didn't manage to update the storage, but we certainly have enough to be getting on with."

"How many *remaining members* are there?" I ask.

"Hmm...with both Eddie Redwood and Frank Tyson dead, that leaves me and two others."

"Harvey Grouder and Melanie Anderson."

Locke turns to Angel and frowns. "How did you know that?"

"Frank Tyson gave away a lot when I interrogated him such as details about how the data was shared among the four of you. In a way, you were the last root to be dug up."

"I...what does that mean?"

"Like you said, Mister Locke, you never reveal your whole hand before it's time. The difference between you and me is I apply that thinking to allies as well as enemies. So, let's just say Harvey, Melanie, and I are acquainted and leave it there. Now, I am going to start working on a few security issues in my own systems. You two can begin reviewing the documents. Oh, and Gary? If I find you haven't pulled the information from the sources I was already tracking, I won't be happy. If that *is* the case, I suggest you correct it. Trying to hide things from me would not be wise."

And with that, Angel walks out of the room, leaving me alone with one of my least favourite people in the world. Before I can take a seat in front of a computer, Locke chimes in, "I don't trust her. She's hiding something."

"I told you before. Everybody is hiding something."

"Yes, but *you're* a PI. Isn't it your job to find out what people are hiding?"

"Looks to me like you're doing a good enough job of that yourself."

"Not in the same w-way, detective. I'm more like a grave robber. I find the things that aren't so much hidden as buried. You find the real secrets."

I roll my eyes at the blatant attempt to butter me up and turn to face a screen. "Whatever you say."

When the silence has hung long enough to make it clear I'm not buying his shtick, he asks, "What do you think she meant by acquainted?"

"You could try asking them."

"But..."

"*Diu.* Let me make this clear to you. I *hate* you. If I could find just cause, I'd kill you right now. All the time we're working together, I will talk to you when necessary. That's it. Now, I'm going to start with the TS Murder Files. You can pick whatever else you want."

*

"Where are you going?" Locke asks, hearing me get out of my chair.

"To tell Angel you were right about this stuff," I reply and walk away before he can ask anything else.

I find Angel one room over, working on her own machine. She swivels the chair around to face me when I open the door and crosses her arms behind her head. "Found something?"

I nod. "Have you got anything to drink? It's hot in here."

She points under the table to the side of the door, and I see a mini fridge. Inside, there are bottles of water. I take one, too thirsty to ask questions she won't answer, and sit down opposite her.

"So?"

"He was right about the TS Murder Files. The information he gathered was fairly in-depth, but I had some other bits to add to it. Don't worry, I checked my surfing was secure using his system first. The case I mentioned before, Roger Watson or Leonard Tomes? Between my own files from the time and the library news archives, I confirmed they were the same person. It looks like *all* of the victims fit a similar profile;

criminals who got away with it and who were murdered brutally by the original Tech Shifters."

"Well, well. What else did you find?"

"The concept of Tech Shifting first got floated in the year 2055."

"That's twenty-five years ago."

"Exactly. The whole thing was tied to a military contract, negotiated by Dean Hollister with the assistance of Gary Locke's father. I doubt it took twenty years to complete the research. It was likely a combination of waiting for the right opportunity to release it and a bunch of red tape that needed to be cut to allow the equipment to be used outside the military. My guess is Hollister had an idea and wanted to renegotiate certain terms of use."

"Given the way it all ended up, it clearly wasn't just the money he'd make from public sales in play there."

I shake my head and take another drink. "No. And it gets worse when you look into the people who carried out the murders on the TS Murder Files. Every single one of them was a death row inmate reported as killed in private executions. The names I knew them by were pseudonyms."

"You sound certain."

"I am. Even if I didn't have the files, I remember their faces, and they are the exact likeness of the people in the archived press reports."

"I'm curious. Given how much is being kept hidden here, why wouldn't the government purge the library archives?"

I shrug. "I can see two possibilities. One is they slipped up and didn't think about scans of physical media simply because newspapers and magazines are so rare now, and the column space given over to the reports was so small. The other possibility is it was intentional."

"Intentional. Interesting. What do you base that theory on?"

"Have you read Casille's book, *Four Steps to Power*?" She nods, and I continue, "He told me once that the book, along with a few other little hints he'd left lying around, were designed to root out potential threats to his position. The odd ally here and there, too, but mostly it's a way to identify risks. This could be the same. The people who look too deeply and put the pieces together are traced and eliminated to keep the biggest secret of New Hopeland from being uncovered."

"The biggest secret we are yet to uncover."

"Yeah. Right now, though, I'm more concerned with why the government would intentionally allow the murders to take place. And they definitely had a part in it. The killers all had government contracts under their pseudonyms, and all with no set job description. I'd love to believe it was all just to take care of people who should never have been let out, but I can't see that alone being the reason. I think the victims were pawns who placed themselves in the firing line through their crimes. Using death row inmates as the killers though? At best, that's an irresponsible risk. I read the reports. Those three were among the worst this country has produced."

"What I'm about to say may seem strange to you, Cassie, but understand I'm talking from experience. These men were due to be executed and were capable of terrible things, correct?"

"Yeah."

"Then perhaps the goal was multifaceted here. Tying up the loose ends surrounding the criminals who got away with it was undoubtedly one of them. If Tech Shift gear was always going to be introduced into the military and law enforcement, creating a culture of fear around it would be useful to enhance the effects of seeing a Tech Shifter coming towards you. And those they used? They were due to die anyway. If they were offered the chance to indulge themselves one last time, and go out in a blaze of glory rather than through the chair or the injection? People who have no boundaries are strangely adept at that. Even if it meant their *fun* was constrained."

I narrow my eyes at her. "You've worked with people like this."

"Without reading the reports you found, I could not say for sure, but it's likely. Consider this though. Is it better for the worst out there to work uninhibited, or to be controlled by someone who can direct them towards an overarching goal? In a way, I've probably saved as many lives as I've taken."

I choose to hold my tongue. This is an argument I'm in no mood for. Instead, I ask, "What do we do now?"

"I'll get our colleague in there to set up a proper cross-referencing system for what we find and have him add the library reports to it. I'll review it all myself, too, of course. Meanwhile, *you* can chase up whatever you want in relation to our endeavour."

"In that case, I'm going to go and visit someone. I had another idea regarding the blood."

She smiles. "Told you you'd enjoy it."

*

I enter New Hopeland's most infamous gun shop and am surprised to find Joe Farrah is not only behind the counter but working alone today. "What can...?" He stops when he sees it's me. He considers something and then asks, "What can I do for you?"

Well, now I'm confused. "That's strangely nice for you."

He shrugs. "You don't seem interested in getting the point, so I figured I'd try a different tactic. Sort you out as quick as possible so you can fuck off."

"Charming. No assistant today?"

I had to let him go. For his own safety."

"Things getting dangerous?"

"For him they were. The little prick was stealing ammo. Please tell me you haven't come just to chat about my staff."

"You know, you should try smiling more. It might make you more welcoming."

Joe looks up at me and pulls his lips back into a perfect combination of malice and sarcasm, masquerading as the creepiest smile I've ever seen. *Angel Tanner, eat your heart out.*

"Okay, forget it. You'll scare more people off like that."

He puts the box he was examining down and asks again, "What do you want, Tam?"

"Fine, fine. My current client is being tracked around the city. The problem is, there aren't any visible tails."

"So, they're using the city camera system. Wouldn't be the first time that's happened."

"Agreed. But they know *exactly* where she is."

"How do you know that?"

"They call and message her, telling her things like where she's passing, what she's wearing, and exactly when she stops."

"Could still be the cameras."

"No. They're too accurate. Even when she goes out of sight of a camera, they can tell her when she stops and goes, and where she's standing. Unless there's a whole army of people who are very good at not being seen and following camera paths, there's something more going on."

"An army, huh? Maybe she's as likeable as you?"

"Well, thanks for that."

"Look, Tam. I don't care about your client. Unless she's a customer, and what's happening affects her money-back guarantee, I don't see why I would."

"I'm not asking you to care, Joe. I'm asking for help. Do you have anything here that would let someone track a person with such accuracy?"

"Plenty. That shelf over there."

I follow his point to a shelf of ankle cuffs, and the sorts of things that have large flashing lights on them. I shake my head. "She's not an idiot, Joe. She'd notice if someone slipped something so obvious on her. I'm thinking smaller."

He gives me a disgruntled sigh and grabs a catalogue. After flicking through some pages, he stops and turns it to face me. I scan the page and shake my head again. "These are also too noticeable. I mean, maybe if they could sneak something like this one into her shoe or something, but I doubt they'd manage it. Is there maybe something too small to see immediately? Maybe something you could inject into someone like Angel Tanner was doing during the LV case?"

Joe narrows his eyes and asks, "What exactly are you getting at, Tam?"

"I don't know, really. I was just thinking. Theoretically, could you have a tracker so small you could get it into someone's bloodstream?"

A slight tenseness comes across Joe's face, and when he replies, he speaks slowly, picking his words deliberately. "Nothing I sell would work like that."

"No? Too costly?"

"No. Nothing so small would be workable as a long-term solution. Even if you had high grade military stuff, it would take a pounding in the human body. A single tracker would be too fragile and need replacing after a few months."

I give him a disappointed look and say, "It was just a thought. Maybe I'll give the Ping Box another try near her clothes. Thanks, Joe."

"You're welcome."

I give him a casual wave and leave the shop, making a point of glancing over my shoulder as I enter my car. Joe has already called someone and looks pretty mad. *Got you.*

I pull out my phone and hit Angel's number. "You catch any of that?"

"Nope. Joe Farrah's cameras aren't on the network."

"That's...surprising. Anyway. We need to talk."

*

"I should have guessed," I say, stepping into the apartment Angel told me to head to. "The floor above my place puts you close enough to get in and out to set up all that stuff with the holographic projector."

"It *was* useful for that. I don't come here often though. With the way things are looking, I need to move around a little more than I'd like, but I try to spend most of my time at the warehouse. If nothing else, keeping an eye on our pet revolutionary is important."

"He's not *my* pet."

She smiles. "Regardless. This is where I come to recharge my batteries. Speaking of which..."

Angel flicks a switch on what appears to be an oversized wireless charger and then sits down on a chair next to it. "There's more water in the fridge."

I grab a bottle and take up residence on another chair. "You've actually got a pretty nice place here. It's basic, but there's everything you'd need if you were a real person."

"I'm less flashy than my sister but yes. It keeps up the pretence. Now, you said we needed to talk?"

"Do you know for certain what the blood is being used for?"

"Yes. So, what did you find out from Joe Farrah?"

"I ran a scenario by him. If someone is being tracked to the degree it appears, then it seems unwieldy for the watchers to simply deploy a massive team. Especially if they need to track more than one person. So, I put it to him that a small tracker could be injected into someone and hang around their bloodstream."

"And what did he say?"

"Something so small wouldn't work because it would break up inside the person and need replacing every few months. The thing is, he was really cagey about it. And when I left, he immediately made what looked like a pretty angry phone call. Given how much he hates that the Kings were working with me, I'm almost certain he was calling it in. Which means there *is* something in the blood."

Angel gives me a round of applause and a wide smile. "I knew you wouldn't disappoint me. You are correct, yes. When you go for your annual check-up, they take a sample of the blood and provide you with a new set of nanochips with the regular vaccinations.”

“Do the doctors know what they’re doing?”

“They’re highly trained professionals, so yes. In terms of this though? No. The vaccine sample has a bar code on it that gets scanned and matched to your record, and the data is pulled automatically by the government databases, tying up the nanochip reference with the one assigned to that particular sample. Harold checked one of the samples just out of curiosity to see what exactly citizens were being vaccinated against and found the nanochips by accident. It was luck on our part, but it did give us a starting point to work from.”

“That makes sense. It leaves us with another problem though.”

“Which is?”

“If I’m right about Joe calling it in, then the Four Kings of Utah have a hand in the tech. Which means the government is not only responsible for the TS Murder Files, but the whole criminal culture of the city. Nothing else makes sense. I was outright told that most people who discover Casille’s secret are killed, and there’s no way the government wouldn’t notice people meeting him and going missing. Especially as those most likely to find out would be those with access to the monitoring files, and if one of them wound up disappearing, they’d *definitely* notice. Not to mention Casille’s complete lack of convictions.”

She sighs and smiles. “I’m glad someone else thought of that too. It means I was right to take the action I did with his father, Arthur.”

“Feeling guilty?”

“Not at all. But it would have been a waste if it turned out I was wrong. He was a useful man in many ways. This link means the information I found was correct. And that I will likely become a target again. Unless this all works.”

“The problem is, if we’re right, then it also means they’re going to have started tracking *me* now.”

“I wouldn’t worry. Once I was sure you were on board, I altered your government files. Right now, if they *are* tracking you, they’re actually following one of your neighbours. It won’t work forever, which is why I’m going to be making changes again soon, but it’ll work for now. I’ve done the same with Locke.”

“What about you? When you took on the role of Nurse Bridges, wouldn’t you have had a medical?”

"Of course. And Harold carried it out in order to avoid the unnecessary discovery of my internals. The nanochips were also real, but I took care of it before I started following Angela."

"Took care of it how? More data altering?"

"You don't need to know. The key point is I'm not being tracked. Now, here's a question for you. If this tracking tech is in place, why don't the police use it to hunt down wanted criminals?"

"Before you mentioned how it works in the hospitals, I would have said criminals don't adhere to the health checks. Now, I'm thinking they don't know." I pause. "Can I ask you something?"

"Of course."

"You targeted a lot of people during the LV case. How many King's Guard are there?"

"The majority of the people Harold and I went after were normal people, used as pawns to hide what we were doing. The actual King's Guard were the main targets, though, so, let's see...excluding you, there were five. Devin Carmichael, Donal O'Brien, Ethan Cobalt, Joe Farrah, and Rebecca Hanson."

I finish my water and shake my head. "I was told Hanson *isn't* King's Guard. She's...there's no way."

Angel laughs. "Do you really think they'd tell you? Look at what we're uncovering here, Cassie. Lies buried beneath more lies. If you need proof, then look at Hanson's record. Since she got here, she's been involved with a number of high-profile cases that should have been problematic for the Kings but turned out not to be. She got *lucky* with what cases she was handed and rose through the ranks at an accelerated rate. And yet she refuses to take a promotion, simply because it would likely mean her moving away from New Hopeland."

"That doesn't necessarily prove anything. Besides, I'm certain Captain Hoover isn't King's Guard, and he'd be responsible for what cases she got, *and* has been trying to push her to take the promotion."

"Oh, he absolutely isn't King's Guard. And yes, he has handed her some cases, but a lot of the time, he's simply signed off on her taking cases from other people. Eventually, he'll retire, and *then* she'll take the promotion."

"No. That's still not enough."

"Okay then, how about this? Public records show she used to work in California. She transferred out shortly after Casille di Franco disappeared, and came straight here, to a city which had only just been founded. That's the stuff you can find out yourself. Want to know the interesting part? Her last case down there was to go undercover and try to use Arthur's ties to my organisation to track *me* down. It was her mistake that led to me finding out Arthur was beginning to figure out what I am. That all being said, I *am* surprised Casille is willing to work alongside her."

"Why? Because, if you're telling me the truth, her actions led to his father's death?"

"No. Because she killed his mother. That part *is* in the public records, by the way. Now, why don't you head out? I need to rest, and you're due to meet with said King's Guard member for some training, aren't you?"

*

With them both wearing the same form-fitting tracksuit bottoms and sleeveless tops, it's easy to see that Lieutenant Hanson is not only a little taller than Lori, but clearly more muscular. So, it's hard to fight back my more protective urges when I see her push Lori back against the crash mat leaning against the wall and move her arm across her throat. *Stand down, recruit. All part of the training.*

"Okay, remember. Once I start applying pressure, alleviate, strike, turn. Got it?"

"I think so," Lori replies.

Hanson nods. "Here we go."

A slight choke comes out of Lori's mouth as Hanson steps in. Quick as a flash, though, she uses one hand to push on the elbow of the arm Hanson has against her throat and slams her free hand into Hanson's forehead. With her foe now off balance, Lori turns the hand she'd used to push the elbow, grabs Hanson's face, and pulls while stepping to the side. Hanson slams into the crash mat, trips, and falls forward, bringing the pad down on top of her.

I let the laughter pour out while Lori scrambles to pull the crash mat aside, and Hanson pushes up onto her knees before taking Lori's outstretched hand and getting to her feet.

"Sorry," Lori says.

"Don't be," I cut in. "That was great!"

Hanson smiles. "To be fair, Cassie isn't wrong. That was pretty good; maybe a touch slow, but it worked."

A look of relief spreads across Lori's face then and she asks, "Any advice?"

"I advise that the laughing hyena over there doesn't piss you off. In all seriousness, though, you doubt yourself a little too much. That's the only reason you're a little sloppy with it. Have confidence in yourself, and you'll be smoother and quicker. Otherwise, what you did works fine. If someone corners you like that, you'll definitely get out of it. And if they don't trip like I did, what do you do?"

"Knee to the gut and run."

"Exactly. Want to try again?"

Lori looks over at the clock and says, "I better not. I kinda need to dive out early tonight because work deadlines mean an early start tomorrow." She looks over to me then and adds, "You can stay if you want. I mean, we're meeting up tomorrow night anyway, right?"

"Yup, dinner date of doom."

"Dinner date of doom?" Hanson asks.

"Me and Lori, and my ex and her current," I clarify.

"Ooh, awkward."

"It'll be fine," Lori says and gives me a quick kiss. "See you tomorrow. Thanks, Hanson."

"No problem," Hanson says and then starts dancing around like an arrogant boxer. "Okay then, what do you want to try?"

"Hmm. Actually, there was something I wanted to check with you. Can I?" I signal for her to turn around and she does. I walk up behind her and slowly apply a light rear naked choke without applying the pressure. "It's figuring out how to escape I sometimes get stuck on. Sometimes people sneak up on you without you realising. Usually, I'd say if you can't see, hear, or speak evil, you can still hit it, right?"

I apply a little pressure and place two fingers behind Hanson's head and then use them to tap out a pattern. Dot-dot-dot, dash-dash-dash, dot-dot-dot. *SOS.*

Hanson shifts her weight, does something I don't see with her hands, and then turns and slams me down to the mats. She climbs on top and, while shifting her position, taps my shoulder. Dash-dash-dash, dash-dot-dash, dash-dash-dot, dash-dash-dash. *OK, go.* Then she says, "See if you can get out of this first."

I start rolling underneath, jockeying for position, and tap out another message. Dot-dot-dot-dot-dash, followed by a rough finger drawing of a crown. *Four Kings.*

I manage to get on top and Hanson balls up into the defence position. She says, "Loosen up. Good. Now, what do you think I need to know here?"

"Probably where I'm positioned?"

"Right," she says and then slips towards my voice and hauls me down.

I grapple from underneath and tap out dot-dash, dash-dot, dash-dash-dot, dot, dot-dash-dot-dot. *Angel.* Then I stop fighting, and say, "And now I'm stuck. Where do I go from here?"

"There are always options, but once you have control, you can pretty much guide things. Bring your arm up around me, use the other one to take my arm, and roll." Hanson lets out a grunt as I come down on top of her. "Good. See? From here, you pretty much have control."

I release the hold and say, "Okay."

"Now, as to the chokehold, I've seen you escape it before. Just keep doing what you do."

"I'm still not sure if I get it all right though. And it's hard to know without someone watching." I crack my shoulder out and try to move the conversation in a way that will mask what we're talking about a bit more. "Maybe next time I can try some of it with Lori?"

"Perve."

I smile and shake my head. "Yeah, yeah. But it would be good to have you watch to make sure I'm not slipping up."

"Yeah, don't worry. I got ya."

"It's kinda hard to try out new stuff without someone else to demonstrate on, isn't it?"

"It can be. Want to call it a night?"

"Yeah, I better." I grab my bag and add, "Hey, it's an odd thing to bring up, but I was curious about something. You remember the case I was working a couple of weeks back?"

"Uh-huh."

"I know you mentioned there being a case you wished went differently. You never did tell me which one you were thinking of."

She gives me a cheeky grin. "You're right, I didn't."

I return the grin and, before leaving, reply, "Typical you. Always on guard, eh?"

*

Click.

And there go the lights. And the kettle.

I peer out of the window and notice the power in the whole street is down. "Well, that's just great. How hot is the kettle?"

I place two fingers on the side and pull them away again quickly, hissing at the infernal pot. "Hot enough."

Fumbling in the dark, I somehow manage to pour a mug of coffee and find my way to the couch to brood over what I'm supposed to do about this whole mess. The problem is, I'm still not sure there are *any* good guys in all of this. Which makes it harder to know who to stand with.

Thud.

Looking over my shoulder, I can see someone has pushed something through my letterbox. *Bert didn't react, so it must have been someone we know. Or at least not anyone we know is dangerous.*

I feel my way over to the door and pick up an envelope addressed to...Bert?

Frowning, I open it and pull out a sheet of paper with what feels like a metal disc attached to it. Using my cell phone for light, I notice it looks similar to the communicator Angel gave to me, but it's bigger and bulkier. The note it's stuck to is short.

Stick it in Bert's mouth and make sure he stays close. We'll do the rest. JF+H.

I'm gonna take that as Joe Farrah and Hanson. It appears the King's Guard work quickly. "Hey, Bert. You have a present."

My little gargoyle trundles over, and I say, "Open up." He opens his beak and lets me place the disc inside. It's magnetised, which is useful. Almost immediately after I'm finished, my cell phone goes off. It's a voice message from an unknown number.

"This is Gary Locke. Get back here. Now."

I consider ignoring it for a second and then shake my head. "*Diu.* Come on, Bert. Looks like it's gonna be a late one."

"Caw."

*

"Wait on the roof of the building. Monitor the situation, but only come in if *I'm* in danger. Don't worry about anyone else. Understand?"

"Caw."

"Good boy." I make my way from the car to the entrance, and once inside, I can hear Gary Locke shouting in the rooms at the back of the building. "Idiot."

"There you are," he yells, as he spots me walk in. "Will you please tell th-this madwoman we have a lot of good info here?"

I roll my eyes and speak to Angel without taking my eyes off Locke. "Hey, madwoman. We have a lot of good info here."

"Oh, very funny. We have so much evidence here tying the government to the TS Murder Files, we could actually bring them down. One of you has to realise that, right? Either of you?"

"I've told you," Angel says, her voice full of amusement. "Things will change. We need to be certain before..."

"Before what? Before I can get back out there and do what I was born to do?"

Angel shrugs. "If you like."

"We need to act before they find us. I can make sure everyone knows the truth, but you won't let me out of this damn warehouse. And M-Miss Tam over there gets to lead a normal life. I'm doing all the digging. It's not fair."

"Need I remind you that you're still a wanted fugitive?" Angel replies. "Cassie is not. Her freedom of movement is an asset you simply don't have right now. Not to mention her ties to the Four Kings of Utah. They trust her, and that may prove useful to us."

"They trust her," Locke mocks and then spits on the floor. "But *you* don't, do you? Or you wouldn't be monitoring her so closely. Were you aware M-Miss Tanner here was monitoring your every m-move, detective?"

I nod and cross my arms. "I was, yeah."

Locke's eyes open wide in shock. "And you're okay with that?"

"Not really. But I understand the necessity."

Locke is getting exasperated now and growls, "We're not going to get anything else out of the data I have access to. This is as full a picture as we're going to get."

Angel laughs and walks over to give him a patronising pat on the cheek. He flinches away as she says, "Such a lack of vision. We need to know exactly who is in control before we act. That's what the three of us have to keep searching for."

"Releasing what we have to th-the public will flush them out."

"No," I cut in. "It won't flush them out, you moron. It'll make them burrow down deeper and start running damage control."

Locke throws his arms up in frustration and then freezes. His shoulders start to shake, and a laugh rises to his lips. "Fine. I've already e-mailed my findings to Harvey and Melanie anyway. They'll be expecting us to act, and when we don't, they will. What do you think of that, M-Miss Tanner?"

"Oh, I already know where you sent the information. I monitor all your incoming and outgoing data. Tell me, when they responded to you, did I get their tone right?"

Locke pales and asks, "What?"

"I told you, you are the last root to be dug up. Frank betrayed you all. And Harvey and Melanie? They were quick to sell each other out. People like them are suitable only to be pumped for information and disposed of."

"You...you killed them?"

"Eventually, yes."

Locke turns to me, desperation in his eyes. "I did some digging into one o-of Dean Hollister's business partners, a man who has a fair few government ties of his own. You kn-know Jonah Burrell, right? He used to live with M-Miss Tanner in California. She's not what she seems. Not even close." Neither I nor Angel react and Locke swallows hard before continuing. "She's a ro-robot, Tam. Like that fucking gargoyle of yours."

I nod. "I know."

His eyes go wide, and he yells "Shit," the tears falling from his eyes almost reaching his voice. In desperation, he tries to throw a clumsy punch at Angel, but she's too quick and ducks under it. She wraps an arm around his throat.

Angel pushes her mouth close to his ear and says, "I do so hate betrayal, Mister Locke."

In one swift movement, she snaps his neck and lets his body drop limply to the floor. She looks down at him and then up at me and says, "It's a shame really. His little delve into Jonah's files taught me something about myself. Remember when I said I could always tell when he was lying? 'It must have taken months' is a trigger he used to stop my sensory readings kicking in properly. Looking back at it, he's been using it for years, which means he's hidden a lot more from me than I realised. I've disabled that little feature now. Or I think I have, anyway. If it weren't for supplying me with the trigger, I may have taken more time over his end."

When I don't respond, she gives his corpse a kick and tilts her head towards me, a curious look in her eyes. "You don't seem bothered by what just happened."

"He tried to kill me and my girlfriend, remember? Besides, I didn't kill him, I just didn't try to save him."

"And if he'd tried to kill you instead of me?"

"Then I would have dealt with him however the situation called for. Failing that, Bert would have finished him."

"Oh? Is he around?"

"He's outside. When Locke messaged me demanding I come down here, I figured trouble was brewing. Don't worry, he's under instructions not to act unless I'm in trouble."

"Aww, no protection for me?"

I nod to Locke and reply, "Doesn't look much like you need it."

"True enough. I apologise for the unexpected excitement. You should go and get some sleep. I have a few links here now that can help deal with our former colleague, and you may have a busy day tomorrow."

"What do you need me to do?"

"I want you to see if you can find out anything about the senior members of governmental departments. I can't access their files from here yet, so what we need is to figure out who has been around long enough to likely be involved with what's happening here. I can focus my own searches then."

"Given Casille's role, they may not all be senior in the sense of known pay grade. They could have moved around to where it's beneficial."

"Agreed. That's why it may take you a while to figure out. I will, of course, let you know if I turn up anything."

"Good enough. We'll speak tomorrow then."

Angel waves, says, "Good night, Cassie," and starts searching for a number on her cell phone.

I exit the building and look up to see Bert sitting calmly on the roof, just as instructed. I beckon him down and he jumps, opens his wings, and glides straight onto the car roof.

"God job," I tell him and open the door so he can climb in. Once he's settled, I get in myself and start driving home.

The weird thing is, the only thing I'm upset about right now is not being upset about Gary Locke's death.

Chapter Five

I glance at the clock in the bottom corner of the tablet screen. Two hours to go until I need to head out to meet with Lori. "I can't believe I've spent all day going through this stuff."

"Caw," Bert calls from somewhere in the kitchen.

"Okay, fine," I reply. "I can absolutely believe I've spent all day doing this. And leave the sugar alone."

The silence that follows is punctuated only by the slightly guilty sound of a heavy paper bag sliding back across the worktop. I roll my eyes and go back to the files on the screen. With a weary sigh, I rub my eyes and grumble. "We've got fewer governmental staff than Salt Lake City, but fifty-three-and-a-half thousand people is still far too many to go through, even with automated searches. After you take out the younger ones who *couldn't* have been here at the start, it *still* leaves over half of the total staff. Then there's the ones who have left already."

I pick up the scrap of paper I have next to me and scan the list of names I've made. Two officials were employed when New Hopeland City was founded and have since retired. Another one is still there now. Four more were in New Hopeland and joined the government from other jobs with two having since retired and two still being in place.

"None of you were high enough to have a definite tie-in to what's going on. But like I said last night, high position does not equal high knowledge. Ugh. Why couldn't Locke have done this already?" I drum my fingers on the table and groan. "His laziness made him blind. He was so focused on the government because he thought them being involved at all was the bigger picture and set out for quick hits. So, if something wasn't obvious, he didn't pursue it."

No, that's wrong. You're not giving him enough credit. I get up and head to the kitchen to make another drink, stopping only to pat Bert while he has a staring contest with the cutlery drawer. *What am I going to need to replace this time; forks, spoons, or knives?*

The kettle starts to make its soothing quiet *whoosh* as the water boils. "He *was* focused on the government, but he was desperate to bring them down. Maybe there isn't anything in the files because he checked, and there wasn't anything worth pursuing. I mean, he *did* find out what Angel is, so he wasn't a complete moron." The kettle clicks off, and I pour the drink. "I can't believe I have to say something good about him. *Diu.*"

Sitting back at the worktable, I take a deep breath, hold it, and release. "Okay. Let's assume this is a dead end for now. Let's refocus on the Tech Shifter gear. Computer, open file name 'Hollister contract results historical,' location external media."

"Processing."

The file opens on screen, and I pinch my lower lip while I think. "Computer, advanced document content search. Compare column title item list with...contents of file name 'Tech Shift gear component list,' location external media. Highlight non-matches."

"Processing."

The currently-working-on-your-latest-ridiculous-request logo pops up on screen, and I sit back in my chair to wait. *I noticed Eddie authored a lot of the files relating to TS gear. Locke obviously knew there was a link, but his priority was to prove the monitoring. The push against Hollister was designed to draw that out as his overall goal, and he just played along with Eddie to keep him onside. He would have dug into this sooner or later though. That much is clear.*

"Request complete. Results on screen."

Sorry, Angel. I'm gonna need to risk a net run here.

"Computer, cross-reference highlighted results with internet search 'common uses'."

"Processing."

I wait.

"Request complete. Results on screen."

I scroll through the listings. The contracts mostly relate to larger equipment. It appears as if they can be used in a lot of different things, but almost all are standard components for industrial machinery. In fact, I recognise some of them. The times I've walked around the manufacturing areas for Familiar Enterprises let me get a good look at the machinery. Some of these fit with what I'd expect to find there. Or I may have just seen similar. *He'd only just found the link with Familiar Enterprises when Angel killed him.*

"Computer, advanced internet search. Search news articles and historic staff pages containing the exact terms 'New Hopeland' and 'Jonah Burrell.' Use dates up to...when did FE Ltd. open? Eight years ago? Yeah. Use dates up to 2072 only. Once done, sort oldest to newest."

"Processing...request complete."

The first page of hits is fairly useless, but the right at the top of page two, I find something interesting. An article titled "AI Entrepreneur Joins New Hopeland Elite." The article covers Jonah Burrell, then fifty-one, being hired to work as head of the programming team for the software firm Hollister and Holtz. It notes that, though no official papers had been released, Joint CEO Dean Hollister was impressed when he saw what he described as an "incredible proof of concept" in relation to Jonah's AI work. The aim was to have him assist with an exciting new piece of intelligent security software, built with the capability to learn.

The next interesting hit sees Jonah leaving Hollister and Holtz to focus on his own projects, with the blessing of both CEOs. There are a couple of articles noting rumours that Dean Hollister provided Jonah with a sizeable loan to start the business, but this was denied by both men. The evidence was pretty straightforward: it was leaked that the money used came from another company owned by Hollister. He later pointed out this company was set up to assist with a variety of government projects. The loan technically came from a legally sanctioned business start-up scheme.

"Someone was busy. Okay, now I'm curious. Let's see what Hollister did before New Hopeland. Computer, advanced internet search. Search news articles and historic staff pages containing the name 'Dean Hollister'. Use dates before 2055 only."

"Processing...request complete."

"Computer, scan results and summarise common themes within them."

"Processing...request complete. Dean Hollister is commonly described as a rising star of the business world. He has held outsource roles with at least twenty companies. These roles are listed as intellectual property consultant and contract negotiator. He has been shown to have been instrumental in negotiating a large number of deals for his employers, roughly a third of which are recorded as relating to supply deals with the US government and US military."

"Computer, cross-reference the name of Dean Hollister's employers with file name 'Hollister contract results historical', location external media. Highlight matches."

"Processing."

I down my coffee, confident in what the results will be.

"Request complete. Results on screen."

Sure enough, every company on the list is highlighted. "Computer. Advanced internet search. Confirm current owner and major shareholders for all highlighted results in file name 'Hollister contract results historical,' location external media."

"Processing...request complete."

Okay. So, some of the companies have been swallowed up by others, all of which are also on the list. Dean Hollister owns every single one of them. And Jonah Burrell holds shares in all of them. Well, isn't that interesting.

"Computer, save results from all requests made within the last hour to external media, new file, name 'Hollister Burrell.' For internet searches that have not been summarised, a link to the results and a copy of the articles opened by user Cassie Tam will be fine."

"Processing...request complete."

I turn the tablet off and take out my cell phone and then send a short message to Angel.

Dead end on government officials. Found links for Dean Hollister and Jonah Burrell. Going out soon. Will show you tomorrow.

I sigh. "I think I could do with the dinner date of doom now."

*

"You're nothing like what I was expecting is all," Jody says, smiling at Lori. "I mean, the whole Tech Shifter thing? I kinda thought you'd be, I don't know, wilder, I guess?"

"Oh, for fuck's sake," Charlie says, and buries her face in her hand.

"You know we're not really animals, right?" Lori replies, sporting a bemused grin.

"I know, I know, but I mean, you feel like you are, right?"

Charlie takes a big mouthful of white wine from her glass. She's beginning to look exasperated.

"I suppose that's...how do I put this?"

"Can I try?" I ask, and Lori opens her hands let me know to go on. "For Lori, Tech Shifting is an escape. When she does it, yes, she enters a headspace where she can immerse herself in the role, but generally speaking, no, she doesn't think she's really an animal. Is that about right?"

Lori smiles and nods. "Very good. That's much better than you would have managed a few months back."

"Well, okay, but what about..." Jody begins.

"No," Charlie cuts in. "That's enough inappropriate questions. Honestly, Jody, sometimes you're cuter when you *don't* open your mouth."

"I'm curious is all. You see all sorts of people at the clubs, but I'm not in the best position to chat, ya know? The DJ booth is like its own set of shackles in a way."

"Well, it's good you're open to things," Lori says. "Seriously, though, not everyone is as laid back as I am. If you'd asked me at a club, I probably wouldn't have been either."

"Oh, right. Sorry."

"Anyway," Charlie says, trying to steer things back on track. "So, what are you up to right now, Caz? You haven't stopped by in a while."

"Yeah, it's been pretty busy. Like the last month, I've dealt with a stalker and a workplace harassment case. Lori helped with that last one."

Charlie turns to Lori, and the smile she gives her is one full of respect. And maybe a little relief too. "Well, good. I'm glad Caz has someone who can help her out a bit. You be careful though. Once she starts getting you involved, it's a slippery slope. You'll be stuck undercover before you know it, and after that, who knows what she'll have you doing."

"I kinda was undercover," Lori replies with a giggle. "But that was enough for me. Obviously, I'll help Cassie when I can, but I really couldn't do what she does. She's something special."

I blush and can't think of a suitable reply, so hide in my wine glass instead.

"Excuse me," the waiter says. "I have your desserts. Let's see. Mississippi Mud Pie?"

"Here," Charlie says.

"Two Black Forest Gateaux?"

"Mine," Lori and Jody say in unison.

"So, yours must be the butter tart."

"Must be," I say, and tuck right in.

"Slow down, Caz. It's not gonna run away."

"Mmm. It's just *so* good."

A quirky little melody plays out, and Charlie makes a quick apology and pulls her cell phone out of her bag. "I better take this," she says and then answers it at the table. "Charlie, go…okay, so everything's set at the usual place…? Good. It'll be done by morning then. Let me know if there are any issues."

Charlie hangs up and I raise an eyebrow at her. She catches my eye, and it's quite clear she knows I have a good idea what the call was about. *That's not good. The timing is too close.*

"Work again?" Jody asks.

"Afraid so," Charlie replies.

"Sounds like you've been busy too," Lori adds.

"You *could* say that. Has Caz told you what I do?"

"She has, yeah."

"And it doesn't bother you?"

"Not really. Does it bother you that, as a member of the press, I could be secretly recording everything for a high-end scoop?"

Charlie laughs and continues, "Well, you'd be on to a goldmine if you recorded me at the right time. Me and the other Elites have been working on some stuff that could make us a lot of money. Like, set for life stuff if it all pans out."

"And she won't tell me a single thing about it," Jody says.

Charlie puts her arm around her and kisses her forehead. "This one needs some secrecy. Besides you don't like it when I talk shop."

"I don't mind really; I just worry about you."

"Trust me. If everything works out, you'll never have to worry about me again. You can thank Caz for that too. I'd have never stumbled into this one if she hadn't nudged me in the right direction."

"Oh?" Lori says.

I frown. "I'm guessing this has something to do with the Malcolm Castleford case?" She brings her wine glass to her lips and points at me with her free hand, confirming I'm right.

Lori frowns. "When you found Fish?"

I turn to Lori and say, "Yeah. Remember how I said Castleford was working on some dodgy stuff outside the dog fight? Well, it goes pretty deep. I've made a point of not digging more than I have to with that one."

She eyes me curiously. "Don't you want to be set for life too?"

"I don't want to *end* my life. That's the problem."

"What?" Jody says, panic not so much creeping into her voice as pouring out of it.

"Well, thanks for that one, Caz."

"*Diu*. Sorry. I wouldn't worry, Jody. Charlie and I are in different worlds, eh? She's actually in a much better place to take advantage of the situation than I was."

"Why do I keep ending up with people like this?" Charlie laments, shovelling more cake into her mouth.

Lori laughs. "Honestly, Cassie, sometimes you are far cuter when you *don't* open your mouth."

*

"So, how are you feeling?" I ask Lori as we head to my car.

"Hmm?"

"Well, I know you were a little...uncertain...about tonight. It was you who came up with the name 'dinner date of doom.' I just embraced it. And when we went in, you were doing that thing where you tense up because you're nervous. You didn't look too happy when you first saw Charlie either."

"Someone's been paying close attention to things tonight."

I shrug. "It's in my nature. So. Come on. Talk to me."

"Well, after seeing her up close, and seeing how comfortable the two of you are around each other, I would say...I'm maybe a little jealous. You can tell you know each other well."

"Oh."

She squeezes my hand. "It's not a bad thing, Cassie. I stand by pushing you to reconnect with her properly. Honestly, with the amount you went on about her at our first date, I needed to know for sure you weren't still too hung up on her."

"I wasn't that bad," I reply, but I know I was.

"Weren't you? Must have been someone else who could barely start a conversation without bringing her into it."

"Okay, okay, so I was a terrible date."

"I wouldn't say that. I came back for more, didn't I? And after tonight, even with the jealousy, I do feel pretty secure. For one, even if you *were* still into her, Charlie and Jody are clearly crazy in love. The little things they do give it away; the glances, the shared jokes, all the warm fuzzy stuff.”

“Now who’s paying close attention to things?”

Lori gives me a playful punch in the shoulder. “Meanie. It was you I was paying the most attention to though. And do you know what I saw?”

“What?”

“That you *do* clearly care for Charlie. At a guess, I’d say you still have some fond memories about her too. But. And this is the important bit. You look at her in a very different way than you look at me. I was happy to see that.”

I lean a little closer while we walk, and briefly rest my head against hers. “Of course, I do. Yes, I do care for her, and yes, we did have some happy times. Where I’m at now is different. In a good way.”

“Good. They both seem nice, anyway. Don’t expect us to be instant best buddies or anything, that would be weird, but they’re welcome to visit, or to join us on another date. If nothing else, it’d be interesting to see what else Jody can come up with to put her foot in her mouth.”

I laugh. “She has no filter, does she?”

“None at all. Hey, is that Bert?”

We reach my car and, yes, Bert is indeed perched on the roof. Judging by the chunk of patterned material in his beak, someone must have gotten a little too close. “Spoils of war?”

“Caw.”

“He’s been quite protective of late, so I’m letting him stick close. I thought it would stop him being destructive, but it looks like he found a new victim. Let’s see how he’s doing…” I pull up an app on my cell phone which tells me his battery is at about 50 per cent. “He should be fine to get back without needing to hitch a ride. I’ll send him off to charge himself, and then we can head back to yours?”

“Sounds good,” Lori says, and walks around to the passenger side.

I tap a few things into the app, and Bert glides off. He’ll go home, but he has another stop to make first. The wording Charlie used was important. “Everything’s set at the usual place,” and “it’ll be done by morning.” When she was with me, she was open about a couple of the side businesses the Elites run. But when one of us had a client there, she used those exact words when confirming they were disposing of a body. Bert is going to check that out for me. The thing is, they often didn’t get rid of it straight away. They hid it in case something happened, and it became clear that the body turning up would be better. They only left it a day though. If I'm right, the timing, combined with the fact there's a dealer tunnel under Angel's base of operations, would mean they're getting rid of Gary Locke.

Here's hoping Bert gets there, and the building's closed.

*

Bert's app sends an alert to my phone just as I finish tidying up Lori's kitchen. She's showering, and it was my attempt at a nice surprise. Born romantic, me.

I open the app and check out the recording Bert has sent. He was a little way from an old, rarely used building. The lights are on and there's smoke rising from it. "Looks like the crematorium is in business. *Diu*, Charlie. I really hope this doesn't mean what it looks like it means."

"Hey, Cassie," Lori calls. "Can I show you something?"

"Coming," I say, and hit the button to send Bert home to charge. Lori sounded a little nervous. That extra wine we had once we got here did seem to push her over the edge a little. I wonder what she's up to.

"Check this out," she says as I enter her bedroom. She's fiddling with a new chest of drawers, sitting snug against the wall on the left side of her bed.

"That's a change from the bedside table. What's in it?"

"Have a look."

I walk over and pull out the four drawers one by one. "It's empty."

She giggles and lets herself drop into a sitting position on the bed. She kicks her legs playfully. "Very observant."

"Do you...need some help putting some stuff away?" I try.

"I *was* hoping you'd be able to help with that."

I smile and shake my head. "Okay, ya drunk. So, where's the stuff you want in there?"

"It's...You stay over quite a lot, right? So, I was thinking, why not get rid of the little table, and you can...uhm...maybe leave some spare clothes here? Like, I know you won't need all four drawers or anything yet, but it'd save you having to keep bringing a change of clothing with you."

"Yet?" I say, a wide grin rising with the blush.

"What? No. I meant...I wasn't suggesting you...Uhm. I think I might be drunk, you know."

She collapses onto her back, and I flop down beside her, my face turned to hers.

"I'd love to," I say, and Lori scoots closer to rest her head on my shoulder, breathing contentedly.

*

"What's this in aid of?" I ask, taking a plate of freshly cooked pancakes from Lori.

"Well, I felt a little guilty about having to get drunk to offer you drawer space. Plus, you cook breakfast more often than not when you stay, so I figured it was my turn."

"You're sweet. How long have you been planning to give me storage?"

"I've had the chest of drawers flat packed for a little over a week now. Yesterday seemed like the right day to put it together."

"Yeah? How come?"

"We had the dinner date of doom. The way I saw it, if it all went well—like it did—it would reaffirm how much I like having you around. And if it turned out you were totally still into Charlie and just using me as a stopgap until you can get her back, I could use the extra space for some retail therapy."

I stop midchew and turn around but go straight back to eating again when I see the mischievous glint in her eyes. "You had me going for a moment there."

"You're too easy. Listen, I'm gonna need to head out soon. I'm due to cover some rally outside the prison, and I need to check in early with the rest of the team."

"No problem," I reply, and shovel the rest of the pancakes into my mouth. "I need to get going too. This current case is keeping me tied up a lot."

"You never did tell me what this one is about exactly."

"For now, I really can't. Maybe once it's done."

"Well, as long as you're keeping safe, it's fine."

"As safe as I can be," I say.

*

The drive to Angel's warehouse gives me time to think things through. I'm not going to mention the Dealers yet. Bert's only monitoring audio as far as I can tell, so by extension, Joe Farrah and Lieutenant Hanson are also getting nothing but audio. If I don't mention what they're potentially up to, then I'm less likely to get Charlie killed.

By the time I arrive, Bert is already perched outside waiting for me. "I really hope you used the open window to get in and out."

"Caw."

"Same as yesterday, okay? Stay put and monitor, no action unless I'm in serious danger."

"Caw."

Inside, Angel greets me with a friendly handshake. She notices me looking at the place where Locke died and says, "See? Told you I'd take care of it. Nobody is going to find him. It'll be like he just disappeared."

"Couldn't have happened to a nicer guy."

"So, you said you found links between Dean Hollister and Jonah?"

"Yeah. I've got the full file here," I say, pulling out a USB stick. "Basically, they've been working together for years. Hollister brought him to New Hopeland to work for Hollister and Holtz back in 2065. He mentioned being impressed with some of Jonah's AI work. He then went on to open Familiar Enterprises in 2072, using a government loan likely funded by one of Hollister's companies. What's more, he owns shares in a number of companies that are not only owned by Hollister but used to employ Hollister as a trade negotiator."

"His AI work. That would be me." She loads up the file on her laptop and starts browsing as she continues, "You know, it's interesting. After you sent that message, I stumbled on something myself. I wanted to look at the founding of New Hopeland. Do you know who the original landowners were?"

I relax into a nearby chair and reply, "Local government?"

"Yes, but they weren't alone. Get this; the buildings where Dean and Jonah live? They purchased the land in 2054."

"One year before the city was built?"

"That's right. I never knew Jonah had any stake in New Hopeland prior to moving here. Here's another one. Have a look at this."

I walk over to the screen and see she's highlighted a couple of the contracts Dean Hollister was involved with negotiating.

She taps the screen. "I recognise all three of these companies. In fact, I've used some of their products."

"What for?"

"I can't remember exactly now. Explosives probably. Or torture tools. The thing is, my own orders with them were made using Jonah's accounts. If Hollister now owns them, and was involved heavily with them back then, it could mean Jonah contacted him to see what the contracts I signed were for. If that's the case, then I may have unintentionally led Hollister to me, and so been responsible for him bringing Jonah here. Looking at where Casille is now, it might be that Hollister finding out about me is what caused Rebecca Hanson to be sent to California, as well as Arthur's eventual betrayal too. I should laugh, really. I may have almost brought about my own downfall without realising it."

"How long ago did you make the orders?"

"The year I took over California—2050."

"Five years before New Hopeland was built and fifteen before Jonah came here. Could they really have been working together that long?"

"To a point. I'm getting the impression Jonah is one cog in a much bigger machine. He's clearly been hiding a lot more from me than I knew. Maybe ever since I was born."

"Born. Seems a strange word given what you are. How old are you, anyway?"

"Chronologically, I'm forty-seven, not that my appearance changes much."

"Forty-seven? I know Jonah had his daughter late in life compared to most these days, but he must have been really young when he made you if that's the case."

"Jonah was very young considering the complexity of the project. Nineteen to be exact. He was a very serious young man, driven and immeasurably proud of what he could achieve when motivated. It all made him very easy to manipulate. Or I thought it did, anyway. No. I did maintain control over him in some ways. But he clearly had enough sense to hide some things...Ah."

I spot the alert in the bottom corner of the screen at the same time as Angel. She clicks it, and a screen pops up showing the outside of the building. Joe Farrah is there, ducked down and on a phone. Angel's lips twitch. She tilts her head back and looks up at me. "Are you armed?"

I draw my Glock, and she nods.

*

From my position behind a stack of disused crates, I've got a good view of the front door. With no current movement, I pull up Bert's app on my cell phone and send him the instruction to stay put. Then, I wait.

Eventually, Joe Farrah enters the building, handgun in hand, and clad in his normal scruffy vest. I'm surprised he isn't better prepared. He keeps his movement slow, scanning the area as she shouts, "Angel Tanner. Cassandra Tam. Get out here, you pieces of shit."

From somewhere across the room, Angel laughs and calls back, "You really don't want me to come out there, Joe. I tell you what, leave now, and I'll show you some mercy."

"Fuck you," he replies and fires a couple of shots off towards where Angel's voice came from.

You can't stay hidden, or Angel will know something's up. I groan at the thought and then stand up and yell, "Joe."

Quick as a flash, he turns and fires off a couple of shots, causing me to duck back down. The bullets audibly hit the crates, at around the height of my head, but nowhere near on target. That *has* to be intentional. A few more gunshots ring out from Angel's direction, and Joe scrambles back behind some debris and reloads. He keeps his eyes fixed on Angel but asks, "What the fuck are you doing here, Tam? Last I checked, you were on *our* side."

"Same as you, Joe. Just working, eh?" I lean around the crates and return the favour, firing off a few shots intended to hit the debris rather than the man. He swings the gun around and fires a single shot into the crate and then stands up and advances towards Angel, pulling the trigger whenever she starts to peer out from behind a bunch of overturned tables.

Obviously tired of waiting, Angel shoves one of the disused lightweight office tables around, causing a loud scrape to echo through the room. Once it's all the way out, she lifts it from the sides and throws it at Joe. It doesn't go far enough to hit him, but the sudden movement makes him duck to the side, and Angel leaps out from behind the now falling office furniture. She swings a kick, smashing her foot into Joe's left hand and sending his gun flying across the room. He rolls with the blow and draws a knife with his right hand. Smoothly, he swings it at the humanoid AI and causes her to drop her own gun.

Joe looks confident as he moves in, but unknown to him, Angel is reaching for another gun stuck in the back of her trousers. I stand up, take aim, and fire off two head-level shots that fly in between Joe and Angel and embed themselves in the tables. Joe leaps back on instinct and, seeing what I did, rolls towards his own gun. He grabs it and tries to drive Angel back. They both take a direct hit in the arm, and stumble.

I swing past the crates and run in just as Angel starts to steady herself for another shot. I tackle Joe to the floor and act as a human shield. We both make a show of struggling for position while Joe moves back towards one of the old machines. As he draws near, he physically kicks me off, a little harder than I'd like, and scuttles back behind the mass of metal. For my own part, I roll to the side, wheezing and coughing from the kick to my gut, and I'm a long way from faking it.

When I look up, Joe has stepped out, gun trained on me but eyes at a point behind me. The moment Angel tries to intervene, he brings the gun up and fires, giving me time to hide again. With things having gone quiet, Joe ducks back behind the machinery. When I look out at him, he's trying to wrap something around his arm to stem the bleeding.

Somewhere back in the direction of the room with the computers in, Angel laughs. "I have to say Joe, it's a pleasure meeting the eyes and ears of the King's Guard again. How were the hallucinations, by the way? Did you enjoy them?"

"Shut up, ya demented bitch."

"Do you know what Joe used to do, Cassie? Before he joined the King's Guard? He worked intel for the military. He was good, too, for a while. See, Joe uncovered some information about a small village being used as a home base for the terrorist organisation of the week. Being an obedient little soldier, can you guess what Joe did?"

"I said, shut up!"

Angel's voice has been moving around. She's trying to throw him.

"Well, Joe made sure the right people got hold of the information, and they sent the troops in. The thing is, Joe was getting tired. He wanted to go home. So, he didn't bother checking his facts enough. The troops, Joe included, slaughtered the entire population of the village. Men, women, and children. And here's the kicker. Every single one of them was innocent. The terrorists had seen the weakness in Joe's resolve and set him up, all with the intent of damaging the image of the US military in the area."

Joe slams his fist against something.

"Joe was discharged due to the effect the event had on him. I mean, what else could they do? He was useless after that, and it's not like his reputation was worth much then either. But I was curious about one thing, Joe. Nobody filmed the incident, so I had to use stock footage from other places. You were there, so tell me this. Was I close? Did I get the children's faces right?"

Joe lets out a guttural cry of rage and steps out into the open. He fires wildly towards Angel's voice. Having gotten the reaction she wanted, Angel leans out and aims a well-placed bullet into Joe's side, causing him to fall and take cover behind the table from earlier.

Leaning out from my own hiding place, I can tell he's hurting. Badly. He's shaking.

Looking around, he spots me gazing over at him. Calming for a moment, he pulls his vest aside, revealing what appears to be a lightweight bulletproof vest underneath. He points to a spot and then nods to my gun. Realising what he wants, I nod back and reload.

Joe yells, "You fucking bitch," and gets to his feet. He starts firing shots roughly at Angel's position, keeping her at bay.

I stand and call out, "Joe."

Joe turns, and I shoot him, aiming as close to where he pointed as I can.

The bullet hits, and he drops, rolling to his stomach so Angel won't see the lack of a major wound.

Joe goes still.

Angel now leans out and, seeing Joe on the floor, not moving, laughs. "Good shooting, Cassie."

I start to respond, but before I can, Angel raises her gun and aims two bullets into the back of Joe's head.

The blood drains from my face, and I'm powerless to stop the vomit spilling out of my mouth at the sight of what's in front of me.

While I try to recover, Angel walks over and casually kicks Joe's corpse onto his back. She pulls his vest aside, revealing the body armour he'd shown me. She looks over to me and says, "See here? Your shot was good, but I thought it was odd he wasn't protecting himself. I figured he was trying to give us a clear target. And he was hiding something. My advice? *Always* go for the head. Are you okay?"

I shake my head and look away from the mess.

"There was someone who worked for me in California who had a similar reaction to an execution. He told me it was due to still seeing the face. It reminded him of the life that had been snuffed out. I've read a few reports about you; Bert has killed for you, hasn't he? The damage he can probably do must make it rough if this is how you react to death. It's no wonder you don't kill often. The truth is, Cassie, there will be more to come. Trust me. You *can* get used to it. If you want to."

She stands up and sighs. "Given that Joe made a move, it's quite clear our location has been compromised. Help me pack some things up. We'll have to move quickly."

I nod mutely and follow her to the computer room, doing my best not to look at Joe as I pass his body. She's right, Bert does make it rough on the rare occasion he has to kill. It's harder when *I* have to, but I can deal with it. The difference is, those people are trying to murder me. Joe wasn't.

*

"Where are we going?" I ask, pulling the car out of the warehouse.

"The apartment. I won't be able to stay there long, but it'll do until my contacts can get me a new place to set up shop."

"Are you going to deal with Joe's body like you did Gary's?"

She shakes her head. "The network is too controlled for him to have obtained anything wirelessly, and I've taken all the hard drives from the base unit machines, so there's nothing the King's Guard are going to get out of this. I'll let them recover the body themselves and dispose of it as they please."

"Doesn't it worry you that they made a move?"

"No. I knew they would eventually. All this means is we need to find stuff out quicker. Honestly, our best bet may be to orchestrate a direct confrontation. Not yet though."

I tap my fingers on the steering wheel, trying to sort my thoughts into a logical order. Finally, I settle on asking, "Was what you said about Joe true?"

"Entirely. All the King's Guard have their little secrets. Not having gained them in New Hopeland, it took a while to find out what some of them were. Other than Rebecca Hanson's, of course. It also meant I had to get creative with how I built the hallucination holograms. Newsreels, movie clips, and the like. The main point is the facts were traceable with a little effort."

I sigh. "Newsreels. Hence the clips you used of my dad. You know, the day he…that was the first time I ever put myself in a position where I regretted my choices."

"Working with me doesn't have to be another one, Cassie. If it helps any, I'll make you a promise, right here and now. When all of this is done, you will be in a better position than you were when you started."

I pull the car up outside the apartment block and say, "Define better."

Angel pats my back and smiles. "Go and get yourself a drink somewhere. Moments like this always pass."

Chapter Six

I'm in too deep. I went too far and got someone killed. Again. Even if he was an ass, he didn't deserve that.

I shake away the thoughts and push my way through the darkened, unassuming door situated halfway down an alley at the southern end of Main Street. It's no wonder people don't know about these places. Without coming down here, I'd have missed it, and even if I had walked this way without looking for it, I doubt I'd have spotted it. If it weren't for Lori, I wouldn't have known about this door at all.

Inside, the alleyway cafe looks surprisingly nice. Dark, sure. And the mass of booths are obviously set up for more privacy than most require, but nice. It's cleaner than The Last Clown if nothing else. I walk up to the bar and, taking Lori's recommendation, make my order. "Green tea."

The bartender nods, and I pay with a banknote. He holds it up to the light and pauses, having obviously read my handwritten request: *Call Devin Carmichael.* He looks over at me, and I say, "Keep the change," and find myself a nice empty booth to sit in.

While I wait, I load up the spare NHC Blend I've been carrying around and open the file relating to Hollister's old contracts. On my regular phone, I access the files relating to the Kitsune case, and scroll down until I find the company names Castleford uncovered during his digging into Casille's accounts. If I'm gonna be stuck here a while, and I'm already too far in, I may as well check everything, right? And the more concrete evidence for a link between Casille and the government, the more certainty I'll have before doing whatever it is I'm gonna do next.

A manual search reveals no full matches, but two partial matches. Both Grant and Thatcher Legal Group and Kendle and Sons Warehouses match up with the name on one contract, Grant Kendle. The name sounds familiar, so I run an internet search and learn he was one of the founders of and original financial backers for the creation of New Hopeland. Though he kept a relatively low profile in terms of public appearances, he was appointed the original mayor of the city, thanks to backing from the then mayor of Salt Lake City. There's nothing too remarkable about him other than that he wasn't a career politician at all; he was a military man who fancied a change of pace.

His public profile states he retired shortly after I arrived in the city and now lives in a mansion out in Salt Lake City. So, I follow the breadcrumbs and run a search for both Grant Kendle *and* Dean Hollister. The only hit is an article talking about the negotiations to provide additional arms for a specialist patrol group, once again with the US military. The picture included with the article shows a younger Dean Hollister, Grant Kendle, and one other familiar face: Ethan "Sunglasses Paloma" Cobalt.

The door swings shut with a loud *thump*, and I look up to see Devin swagger in and head straight for the bartender. He points me out and Devin starts to walk towards me, but I give him a subtle head shake, stopping him in his tracks. He tilts his head and taps one of his ears. I nod and return the gesture, confirming that yes, someone is likely listening. Devin rubs his stubble thoughtfully and then leans back against the bar and turns his head to the bartender. He says something before he strolls out of view and, I'm assuming, into another booth.

The bartender delivers something to someone in the direction Devin went and then stops by my booth to hand me my green tea and a rectangular sheet of glass about the size of my phone screen. Within seconds of him leaving, the glass lights up with the message, *This is a two-way communicator. Don't worry, it's only connected to its pair.*

I place it on top of my phone screen and reply.

Did you recover Joe's body?

We did. What happened?

Angel got him riled up about some military op he was intel for. Apparently, he felt responsible for the deaths in a village.

Yeah, I know about that one. What happened after she brought it up?

Angel shot him. We figured out a plan where I was gonna shoot him in the body armour. I think he planned to ambush her when she got close, but she was too cautious.

So, she shot him in the head when he was playing possum.

Yes.

A pause and then:

How are you holding up?

Not well. If I'm gonna keep working with her, I'm gonna uncover more and more.

How far have you got with that?

Now I pause. After thinking it through, I send:

You mentioned once there was more to why Casille is playing Allen Fuerza than I knew. I have a pretty good idea what the power structure is in New Hopeland now. The problem is, if I've figured things out, then so has Angel.

Okay. Any idea what she's planning?

No. She mentioned orchestrating a direct confrontation, but I don't know who with exactly. It could be Dean Hollister, Jonah Burrell, Casille, or the King's Guard. And she knows all the King's Guard, by the way, so now I do too. Tell Hanson she has some explaining to do if I get out of this alive.

I think I hear a chuckle drift across from somewhere, and Devin replies.

I'll do that. Any other intel you can give us?

Angel has access to whatever monitoring network the government is running and can monitor pretty much everything. Any plan you guys get in place needs to be set up in a way that isn't recorded.

We can accommodate that. Honestly, though, we're kinda planning to follow your lead as far as possible.

I'm not in charge here, Devin.

No, but Angel is. So, following your lead is, by extension, following hers. We can let things get to where Angel wants them and deal with her then. Any idea what her overall goal is?'

No.

Okay. We recovered the communicator from Joe's body, so just keep Bert transmitting. Trust us, Caz. Things will work out.

And with that, Devin gets up and leaves.

*

I open my eyes, and I'm back in my family home. Mom is in the kitchen ignoring me, and I'm in the living room ignoring her. My tablet is in my hands, and I turn it on.

I remember this. I opened the web browser next. But it was wrong.

Sure enough, when I open the browser, my homepage has been changed to a news article about some city in Utah that's going through a huge rise in crime. The city is called New Hopeland, and the local police are struggling to keep up.

I didn't really know too much about the city until then.

We jump to later the same day. I'm looking through some other sites, and the ad banners are showing property in New Hopeland.

That happened a few times.

The next day, now. I'm on the phone to Kirsty Macdonald, one of the cops who stood by me after what happened to Dad. "So you know someone down that way…? Do you think you could get them to put a good word in for me with the Captain…? No, I can't stay here. Not much longer. I need to do something, Kirsty. A change of scenery is just what I need, eh…Okay, thank you."

I'm in New Hopeland. The realtor had just told me about how there are so many housing options available due to a massive turnover in residents. We'd put it down to rising crime. The property we're in is the third one she showed me. Kirsty helped me get fully licensed, and my historical records were enough to secure me the mortgage, though really, I should never have been approved.

Looking at it empty like this, it's hard to believe it would become home.

With Lori, now. "Apparently, Devin knew you by reputation back when you were in Vancouver. He said something about some associates of his knowing about your work or something like that."

*

I sit up in bed, panting heavily, and wipe my brow.

"*Diu.* There's no way. They couldn't have…"

I grab my tablet and start searching for articles relating to housing booms in New Hopeland. There's nothing. At no point in time has New Hopeland ever been officially in a housing boom.

"But when I got here, there really were a ton of houses and apartments available. It seemed like a third of the city was vacant. That can't be right either."

I put the tablet down and try to think things through.

"Could they could access people's equipment outside New Hopeland? Of course, they could; anyone can remotely access anything with the right tools. They knew me by reputation. I shouldn't really have been approved for a mortgage on this place, but I was. And whenever I run low on funds, something comes along paying just enough to keep me going for a while longer. Either I've been very lucky, or they headhunted me and have been watching me all along."

I shake my head.

"No, headhunted isn't right. Handpicked and influenced maybe, but I was not meant to be King's Guard. Maybe a back-up plan—someone they could hand stuff off to without me knowing?"

I drop back onto my back and stare up at the ceiling. That's when it hits me. "I'm overlooking the important part of the dream. What really happened to the people who left the city?"

*

Ordinarily, a shower and drowning in coffee would make things more bearable. Not today though; everything is getting on top of me. In truth, if what I'm thinking is right, I'm not certain anymore which side I come down on. *No, you know you aren't on Angel's side. You just don't know if you're on the government's side.*

I make it out of the elevator just as the door to Angel's apartment shuts, and to my disappointment, it's not Angel who's leaving but the person I hoped to keep out of this. "Hi, Charlie."

"Caz," she says, sporting a cheery smile. She nods over her shoulder to the door and adds, "She said she thought you'd be dropping by. I was coming to grab you, actually."

"Oh? So, is this what you were talking about when you said set for life stuff?"

"Yeah. Who'd have thought *he* was the one behind the Four Kings?"

"It was...a surprise. If you figured that out, did you make contact?"

"That was a tense night. Still, it put us in an interesting position. When our mutual colleague in there got in touch too, I couldn't believe it. This is a chance to change everything."

"And Gary Locke?"

"I thought you'd pick up on that. Yes, that was us."

I close my eyes and sigh. "I hope you know what you're doing, Charlie."

"More than you realise," she replies and gives the door a knock.

It cracks open, and Angel peers out. When she spots me, she finishes unlocking it and steps outside. "Are we ready to go?"

"Go where?" I ask.

"You'll see," Charlie says and starts leading us away while Angel piles me up with a couple of extra bags.

As it turns out, there's access to one of the dealer supply tunnels, a complex run of secret underground corridors used to move drugs, a few blocks from my apartment. Eventually, we come out into a small room fully decked out with carpet, chairs, and proper lighting. "What is this place?" I ask.

"One of our rest points," Charlie replies. "You can walk the entire length of the city and be a little tired, right? Try doing it while carrying supplies. There are a few of these spots dotted around. The other Elites know what it's going to be used for, so you won't be disturbed. Outside, turn right and keep walking. There's a manhole opening to another warehouse if you need a quick escape. No ladder, though, so be ready to climb."

"Got it," Angel says. "Well then, we better get set up."

"Gotcha. Give me a call if there are any issues. And Caz? Don't worry. Things will work out; for both of us."

Charlie leaves, and once I'm certain she's out of earshot, I turn to Angel and ask, "How much does she know?"

"Right now? The identity of the Four Kings and that Casille essentially controls crime in the city. I haven't told her anything else."

"Don't you think you should?"

"I will when it's time. Unless she does something silly before then, of course."

"Meaning?"

"Meaning I believe the Dealers may yet betray me. It's risky working with them given they've met with Casille, especially as, unlike you, they negotiated their position upward. That's the advantage of having a gang of mercenaries at your beck and call, I guess. Right now, I'm keeping an eye on things and riding the wave of resources."

"Even if she does move against you, I won't let you kill her. You know that, right?"

Angel grins, baring her teeth, but without looking at me. She's like a lioness who knows she could spring whenever she wants. "If that's the case, Cassie, then you had best hope she doesn't betray me. I'd hate it to ruin our partnership."

"Noted."

Angel turns her laptop on and starts rearranging some of the other computer equipment. "So, you were quiet on the way down here, and the first question you asked me was what the Dealers know. Given your natural paranoia, I'd say that means you've found something but weren't sure whether to mention it or not."

"I might have. When I first came here, it was in the middle of a housing boom, but there's no trace of it anywhere online. The governmental monitoring offices won't give me access to the files for each and every past citizen without me having just cause, but I think it's worth looking into."

"Oh? And why's that?"

"With the amount of links Hollister has to seemingly everyone in a high position in the city, the set-up of the TS Murder Files, and the fact he and Jonah bought land here before the city was built...I'm beginning to wonder how many of the original citizens were legitimate homemakers."

"Hmm. What set you off down that path?"

"I was told at least one member of the King's Guard knew about me before I came here. It wasn't until days before I moved that I really knew much about the city, and even then, it was only because of online adverts that started appearing for me when I surfed the web. The thing is, at the time I didn't meet the criteria for a mortgage, but they gave me one, and whenever things get tough, a case drops into my lap that fixes everything. I think...I may have been *brought* to the city. If I can read the records, I can at least figure out if the housing boom was natural or not."

"Interesting. That would mean there may be more like you. Well then. Switch on the computer over there."

I follow her gesturing thumb and do as I'm told. When the computer finishes loading up, Angel joins me and places a briefcase on the table next to me. She opens it, pulls out a small metal sheet with a USB attached to the bottom, and plugs it into the base unit. The briefcase also contains a number of vials of blood, and she selects one marked with the initials RH. Using a pipette, she drips a drop of blood onto the sheet, and says, "Give it a minute or two."

Time drags on, and eventually, the screen flashes up a *Welcome, Rebecca Hanson* message and a bunch of file folders. Angel starts clicking through the folders and says, "It's amazing what you can access with the right blood, isn't it? Ah, here we go. These relate to housing. I'll leave you to find the right time period. After that, you can just get the computer to cross-reference names the same as you normally would. We have net connectivity, but with enough layers of security to mask us so long as we don't overdo it.

"So, work quickly. Got it."

It doesn't take long to find the names and addresses of people who moved within three months either side of my arrival. I'm on the list too. A good chunk of the information I was looking for is even included in these files. The bits I can't find, I set the computer to locating, and in under ten minutes—because Angel apparently splashes out a good deal more on tech than I do—I have it.

Once I've finished reading through all the information, I call her over and run through my thoughts. "I reviewed a six-month period, and it looks like at least one third of those who left New Hopeland had civil service jobs while they were here then moved on to high paid jobs in other cities but within in the same employment sector. Those coming in were a mix of new starters and transfers from outside. A small number of people held more standard jobs; mechanics, postal workers, and so on. Some moved within the city, others move away. The majority, though, couldn't be found. They left, allegedly, but there are no mentions of them anywhere online."

"Social media?"

"Even there. The weird thing is, a lot of them don't even have profile photos on these files, so I can't run an image search for them."

"Pseudonyms."

"That's my thinking too. I had a brief look back and it does seem like there's been periods of mass property shifting every year over the last seven years. Both sales and rental properties come into play here. It's like a refreshing of the guard. Is there anything on here that goes deeper? Maybe we can find out who some of these people really are, or why I'd be manipulated into moving to the city?"

"Probably. This is about as much as we can access with Rebecca Hanson's blood though. I suspect we'd need someone far higher up in the food chain to go deeper." She clicks her tongue and says, "With everything we've uncovered so far...You know what this points to, don't you?"

I nod. "New Hopeland was built for a specific reason. It's not a real city. It never has been."

We sit in silence for a moment. When it becomes clear she isn't going to say anything, I turn to face Angel and ask, "So, what do we do with this?"

"Tell me, Cassie, what do you think my overall goal is here?"

"I have no idea. You haven't told me anything about what you want to achieve."

"I'm a careful person. I saw you as a potential ally for two reasons. One, you were already established here and had links I could use if I got you on side. And two, you've been used and screwed over by the King's Guard, who've forced you into life-threatening positions without forewarning. Even so, I needed to be sure I could trust you before I gave too much away."

"And can you trust me?"

"I can trust in the way you act. That's good enough. What is my goal in New Hopeland? Change, I guess. The full extent of the change, I'm not sure yet."

"Change, eh? Everything we've seen points to this system that's in place being so far ingrained in the city that it's...it's like the city's central nervous system. Bringing it down in any way would be difficult at this point."

"I quite agree. We're also missing an important piece of information: what Jonah's AIs have to do with it. My existence brought Hollister to him, and now he has a new one to play with. There's no trace of the project's aims in the files we have. I know, I've checked. Still, we can always ask him. Yes. Tonight, in fact. Once we know that, we plan the big attack."

*

"How are you feeling?"

I shrug. The voice changer in the mask makes my words sound strange to me as I answer, "The LV suits are actually pretty comfortable. If only I wasn't worried about you controlling me, eh?"

She rolls her eyes. "I already told you, I'm not going to do it again. It was necessary when we broke Locke out, but not now."

"Here's hoping. Any luck with the lock?"

"No, not yet...you know what? Screw it." Angel lifts her leg and slams her foot down hard on the lock, once, twice, three times, stripping it away from the wall. I guess we'll never make locks that are actually secure.

With the door open, she walks inside and slams a fist into the control panel to the right of the door, cutting the alarm that's blaring. Next, she grabs a decorative pot from a small table and throws it at the security camera.

"What happened to being quiet?" I hiss, walking in behind her.

"Like I said, screw it. He'd know we were here soon enough anyway."

Angel stops in her tracks and raises her hand, halting my walk forward. In the darkness ahead, a shadow moves. Slowly at first and then breaking into a dash. Before I can even register what's happening, Angel throws her hand out. There's a *clunk* and then a *thud*, and we're on the move again. On the floor just ahead of us is a pitch-black Familiar in the shape of a Doberman. It looks like Angel used one of her remote disablers on it.

We move into the living room, and Angel grabs the TV remote, and uses it smash another security camera. With no way for Jonah to see us now, she points to the door. I nod and walk over, pressing myself against the wall so as not to be seen. Meanwhile, Angel sits herself down into one of the chairs and waits.

Moments later, the quiet padding of someone sneaking down the stairs makes its way into the room. When the unmistakable sound of a gun being held by a shaking hand joins it, I tense up. *I have to time this right.*

Jonah Burrell steps slowly into the room. He brings the gun up to aim it at Angel. "I know it's you, Angel. You can take off that ridiculous mask."

"Fair enough," she replies, and slowly slides her LV mask off. She drops it down onto her lap, and Jonah steps further into the room, his gun still up.

Seeing my opening, I step to the side, and place a hand on his shoulder. I give him a quick tug. Jonah starts to turn with the pull, and I mirror the movement, bringing my hands into position around the gun as it comes into view. A shot fires, and something behind me smashes. With a twist, I disarm the businessman and then force his arm behind his back and turn him back towards Angel. Upstairs someone screams.

A scream is usually followed by a call to the police, so I'm glad when Angel gets straight to the point. Even if her calmness is far too eerie. "Why did you *really* make Angela, Jonah?"

"Answer her," I say, applying some pressure to his arm. "We know why the city was built."

"Really? It must have taken months to figure that out."

Angel smiles, and even in the dark, the white of her teeth reveals a maliciousness Jonah wasn't expecting. "Yes, it did. Do you know what else took me a long time to figure out? What your trigger phrase is to shut down my ability to tell when you're lying. Just so you know, it won't work anymore."

"That's...how did you...?"

"Quit stalling for time. I know full well your wife up there will have called the police by now. I'll ask you again. Why did you really make Angela? I know it has something to do with this city."

"I really don't know. I got the contract, and no other information."

"Oh, Jonah." Angel rises to her feet and stalks across the room. She brings her face close to his. "One. You're lying. Like I said, I cut your control over that little quirk you built into me. Two. Cassie and I really do know why the city was built. We also know how far back your relationship with Dean Hollister goes. Three. I'm beginning to get *really* pissed off now.

"After all that honesty I've afforded you, you're still trying to lie to me. So, let me give you some more honesty. In a moment, I'm going to ask you a question. If you don't answer it, then I swear to you, I will kill your wife and your daughter. I will make it slow, and I will make sure they are aware of every excruciating little moment of their life that drips away. It won't be today, but it *will* happen. Now. Why. Did. You. Make. Angela?"

I can feel Jonah's heart quicken. He's taking her seriously. "Okay. Okay. She's being groomed to be mayor. I don't know when it's supposed to happen. Just that it's the overall goal."

Angel searches his eyes and smiles and then gives him a playful pat on the cheek. "See? Was that really so hard?" She looks at me and says, "He's telling the truth. Let's get moving."

I turn and shove Jonah back into the hallway he entered from and then dash out with Angel. By the time we've reached the car and are speeding away, sirens are coming in from behind us. I kill the lights and glance at the rear-view mirror, watching as the lights turn off towards Jonah's house. "We got lucky."

"Never undervalue luck, Cassie. What do you think about Angela's future role?"

"I don't know. I guess they want someone easier to control than a regular human."

She laughs. "Because that worked out so well for Jonah with me. Though I suppose he did have his sneaky little vocal trick. It does mean the founders of New Hopeland are looking to increase their level of control over the city in the long term though. And in a way they're confident is foolproof. What we need now are the plans for Jonah's house. No, all of Lambert Drive."

"Why?"

"Because Jonah bought the land before New Hopeland was built. I think there's more there than we're seeing."

"I don't suppose they're in Locke's files?"

"He doesn't have a single set of house plans in there. Given he didn't figure me out until the end, though, what reason would he have to play in that particular hole? No, we're going to obtain those themselves. Or to be more precise, you're going to have to."

"Hang on. Why not use some King's Guard blood to access the records?"

"Because they don't have access to them."

"Really? They've got records of who lives and owns where, but no actual plans?"

"That's right. It makes sense if you think about it; they can access monitoring records because that's all they need. If they need anything else, they can get them. I'm sure. Actually, that gives me an idea."

"I'm not going to like this, am I?"

"Have some faith, Cassie. We're almost done."

"That's what worries me the most."

Chapter Seven

Looking at the New Hopeland Police Station, I can't help but think about how few people inside know what the true nature of crime within the city is. It's scary, really; these are the people sworn to protect and serve, but they don't understand what it is they're protecting or who they're serving.

I shake the thoughts away and start making my way inside only to bump into two familiar people in unfamiliar plain clothes. "Will?" I ask, taking in his shockingly casual shirt and jeans combo. I lean forward and sniff, confirming my suspicions. "I can actually smell the hair gel. You look like a college student."

He laughs and replies, "Today, I am. Forget William Devereaux, my name is Robert Smith. I'm studying for my Medical Technology major. Who knows, maybe I'll find *the cure* for something."

Captain Hoover, also dressed in casual attire, snorts, bristling his ever-impressive moustache. He offers a handshake, and I take it. "William Smith. I let my *son* here pick the names. Last time I make that mistake."

I laugh. "Not into your retro music?"

"No, I am not. If I'd wanted to use old celebrity names, I'd have picked an obscure baseball player or something."

"Oh, come on, Pops," Dev chimes in, clearly relishing his role. "We're going to a karaoke bar. I for one cannot wait to hear about your journey to Bel-Air."

Hoove rubs the bridge of his nose and mutters, "Don't push it or you won't make it to Friday to be in love."

"This is good," I say. "You could take it on the road. Play the lifestyle bars. Earn a few dollars on the side."

"Don't encourage him," Hoove says, though I can see from his smile he's taking it all in good humour really. "What brings you here today?"

"Cheekiness. I'm running low of fuel *and* money, so I thought I'd come ask about a new discount code."

He nods. "Hanson's off doing…I don't know, probably something she shouldn't be. Donal's at his desk though. He should be able to help."

"Thanks, *Will*. I better not keep you chatting; kids can get a bit antsy when they don't get where they're going quick enough, eh?"

"Are we nearly there yet?" Dev chimes in.

"Too right. Catch you later, Caz." As they walk away, I hear Dev say to his *son*, "You know, I used to feel sorry for you. Now I'm not sure how Hanson puts up with you."

I smile and walk inside. Sure enough, Donal O'Brien, Marshal of New Hopeland PD's Tech Shift Division, is at his desk. He seems pretty distracted. Taking full advantage, I quietly slide into the chair facing him and wait. When I get no response, I give an intentionally loud cough, startling him enough to make him physically jolt back. I'm happy with his reaction.

"Jeez, Cassie, ya near scared the life out of me." The normally playful Irish lilt to his voice has been replaced by a weary edge.

"Sorry, couldn't resist. You seem busy."

"Lots of paperwork. Got called out to Jonah Burrell's last night. You wouldn't happen to have heard anything about some trouble up that way, would you?"

I shrug. "If I hear anything worth passing on, I'll let you know."

"Fair enough. So, what can I do for you?"

"I needed a new fuel discount code, and the Fresh Prince sent me your way. Figured we could catch up a little too; it's been a while."

He nods, locks his computer, and rises to his feet. "I'm due a break anyway. I'm the only TS guy in today, so the training room is free to chat. I'll grab you the code from my bag while we're down there."

"Sounds good," I say, and notice him sending a text message from his phone. I choose not to ask about it and instead follow on as he leads me through the station and down to the floor where the Tech Shifters train for duty. On the way, he turns cameras off remotely. "Should I be worried?"

He looks back and I nod to the camera he's just switched off and he says, "Nosy feckers, the staff here. Ever since the LV case, they always get interested when you come in. I figured, if we're gonna chat, we may as well have some privacy. Maybe give them something to gossip about."

"Still, I'm sure not everyone is interested in me. I'm gonna guess you know who's listening in."

He glances over his shoulder and catches my eye. I give a small nod in response and he turns away and sends another text. "Aye. I do that."

We make our way into the training room, and once the cameras are all off, Donal turns to me and asks, "How are you doing?"

"I've had better days. What happened to Joe was…I thought he was on to me, but I wasn't expecting him to turn up like that."

"He wasn't supposed to. His job was to find Angel then wait for further instructions. Honestly, I think he only went in like he did because he was pissed about her using the hallucinations on him."

"He mentioned me speaking to him about that then?"

"Aye."

We stand in silence for a moment, and then I ask, "Can you satisfy some curiosity for me?"

"Sure."

"Were you always pegged for TS gear? Like, from the start, not from the public announcement."

"I was a later recruit to the process, but it was always on the table for me. You managed to dig up that much? Does it mean you know about the way TS gear has been used here?"

Careful wording in case I don't know yet. Clever. "I do. Can't say I'm happy about it either."

He nods. "And does knowing that make you feel any different about Lori?"

"Of course not."

"Good. Other people you care about are a good tool to get you through the tougher times."

"I quite agree."

I spin to meet the smooth voice that responded and find myself face to face with Ethan Cobalt. I think I'll stick with Sunglasses as a name for him. Somehow, it makes him seem less threatening. Or allows me to pretend that's the case anyway.

"Are the tunnels clear?" Donal asks.

"They are," he replies and turns to face me again. "I will keep this brief. Do you know what Angel Tanner's overall goal is?"

"Angel is…strange. Sometimes she trusts me enough to tell me what's happening, other times she's content to test me and have me prove my loyalty. All she's told me is she wants change. Beyond that I don't know."

"Do you believe Casille is a target?"

"I can't be certain. If I had to guess, then based on how intertwined he is with everything, including Angel herself, I'd say it's a good possibility."

"Intertwined with everything," he repeats. "May I ask, how much exactly do you think you know?"

"Too much."

He smiles. "On that, we agree. Has she told you anything that may be useful to us going forward?"

"She wants me to research Jonah's property. What's more, she wants the original plans for the whole street. Even with unrestricted access to the systems you guys use, she hasn't been able to find them."

"That means she's figured out what's beneath his house," Donal says. "She's going straight for the heart."

"Undoubtedly," Sunglasses agrees. "I don't suppose you know her plan of attack and just thought it wouldn't be useful?"

"No. I do know it's going to be soon though. She told me last night we're almost done."

"In a way, that could work to our advantage. If she had no knowledge of the layout of the complex, then her movements would be erratic. But if she has access to the plans, I am fairly certain I can second-guess her actions. Mister O'Brien, please arrange the necessary paperwork for Miss Tam to acquire the plans. I shall begin work on a defence plan."

Sunglasses turns and walks away. He disappears into the back of the station's lower floors. Donal watches him go, then places a large hand on my shoulder and says, "Come on. We'll get you a warrant for the LGKB."

*

I make it back to my car a little slower than I'd like. Part of that was due to making sure I wasn't being followed; I hate being strung along. Part of it was also because I really did need the fuel discount code and was rather insistent on getting it. The car is parked a few blocks away in a public car lot. The second I sit down my cell phone goes off. I hit answer.

"A job well done," Angel says. "I don't expect the prospect of a direct assault to shake either Ethan Cobalt or Devin Carmichael, but it may do the others. Did you hear Ethan? He was *clearly* issuing a challenge there. He can second-guess me, can he? We shall soon see."

"So, what now?"

"Well, they confirmed there's something below Lambert Drive. From the tone of the conversation, we were right that it's important too. The key here is to let them think they hold all the cards; they know where we'll strike, and they think you're still on their side. So, let's get those plans and see what we can find. What's the LGKB, by the way?"

"Local government key building. It's New Hopeland lingo. The governmental monitoring offices, or GMO, do the online monitoring. The LGKB does the real-world stuff, including holding secure planning files."

"I see. You sound *off*. What's wrong?"

"We're about to tackle the King's Guard."

"I promised you you'd end up in a better position than the one you started in, remember? Trust me, Cassie."

"In that, I do. That's the problem though. I've been running possibilities through my head, and I can foresee many outcomes. Some of the King's Guard are my friends. Even with all of this...they're good people. I don't want them to die."

Angel lets out a quiet chuckle down the phone. "I can make you no guarantees on that point. I tell you what. I will let you deal with as many of them as possible, how about that? As far as possible, their fate is in your hands."

"That's about as good as I'm gonna get." I sigh. "I'll get the plans and meet you back at home base."

*

"Oh, hi, Jeremy," I say, surprised to find one of the GMO staff working the desk at the Key Building.

"Hi Cassie. How's Lori?"

"She's good. What are you doing here? I thought the GMO and LGKB had different employment pools?"

"They do," he laughs. "Turns out a *lot* of people have made complaints about the customer service staff here, so a couple of us are helping out while people are retrained."

"Huh. I think a couple of those complaints may have been mine."

"They were. I loved the one about the adviser having an abrasive attitude that made your visit akin to scrubbing your ears with sandpaper."

"Poetic, eh? And entirely true."

"I can imagine. I saw a few of them in action when I made my first stop by. Anyway, what can I do for you today?"

I show him the warrant set up on my phone and say, "I need copies of the original plans for Lambert Drive."

"Fully annotated it says here. So, you'll be wanting the updates showing what was and wasn't built."

"That's right."

"Strange request," he comments, his hands flying over the keyboard. "I suppose PI work can get a bit odd at times though?"

"You don't know the half of it."

He stops typing and says, "Well, that's odd."

"What is?"

"It says there are no digital copies, only physical prints. Must be one of the legacy things they haven't dealt with yet. Not to worry; we'll just photocopy them. I'd normally go and grab those and make the copies myself, but I've sent the request through the internal system. They'll be delivered straight to us in a couple of minutes. Mister Sandpaper is on duty right now, so I thought it would be a nice surprise for him."

I laugh. "You're cruel."

"Sometimes. But hey, you make Lori happy, so I figured you're worthy of some fun."

"Hey, can I ask you something?"

"Sure."

"You said ages ago that Lori helped your family out. What did she do?"

"She hasn't told you?"

I shake my head. "She said it was your story to tell, not hers."

"Oh. Well, I mean, sure. You ever hear the old saying that press photographers have to take the photo first and then help?"

"Yeah. It eats at her a bit, actually, knowing she has to do things that way."

"Well, she made an exception once. My wife flipped her car with our son Steven inside. Lori happened to be nearby doing photography for some political piece and, when she saw what had happened, stopped what she was doing and rushed over. Everyone else froze from what I heard, but Lori? She was straight in there. She got Steven out and then Teri. The car went up in flames before the ambulance got there."

"Wow. It's funny, but she was working with me on something recently, and she was so certain she wasn't brave at all, not naturally. That's incredible though."

"She was working on instinct, she said. She stopped by to check in with us after and even helped out with the immediate costs for the hospital bills. I paid her back once I got paid, of course, but she said she didn't want the bill hanging over us. We've been friends ever since. The kids love Ink, especially our youngest, Ted."

"Ink's really something," I say, smiling. "It's hard to imagine one without the other, isn't it?"

"It sure is...ah, here we go. Thanks, Barry. You remember Cassandra Tam, right?"

"Of course," he says through gritted teeth. "She's one of our regular..."

"Valued," Jeremy cuts in.

"Valued...customers. If you'll excuse me, I have work to do."

He scuttles off without waiting for a response, and both Jeremy and I crack up.

*

Angel slides the paper showing the properties built to the left, lining it up with the original plans for an easier comparison. "So, it says here there should have been twenty-four houses in total."

"That's always been the rumour. Why we only got numbers twenty-one to twenty-four is anyone's guess, but until today, I can't say I ever believed it was anything more than a weird numbering quirk."

"What do you make of the note here?"

"That work was halted due to issues with the foundations? I don't buy it. If that were the case, there would have been more concerns about the four houses that *were* built. On top of that, according to this, the power lines are active. Why do that if you weren't going to make the rest of the street?"

"Exactly. So, here's something. Look at the basic plans for houses one to twenty. Tell me if you notice anything about the rooms."

I start looking over the papers, comparing the different would-be properties. Initially, nothing springs out at me. It's not until I start placing the plans one on top of the other that it starts to make sense. "All the houses are identical in design, but these four are completely different sizes. The original plans show all of the houses as the same size though."

"The layout is odd too. They're single-floor plans for multi-floor houses and have things like kitchens attached to bedrooms. There's no way this is right. Which means they're the plans we need."

I scratch my head and start laying them out next to each other in order. "Given what Sunglasses said, we know there's something under Jonah's house. He outright described it as a complex. And look at this. If the houses are set out in this order—twenty, seventeen, nine, five—then the front and back doors line up, despite being in odd places. Except five which doesn't have a back door."

Angel rotates the plans for the houses to the right, making them start at Jonah's house and then move north rather than follow back along the street. "And if you lay it right next to twenty-three like this, the front door on twenty lines up with the point where the power lines connect."

"The property notes show that, other than Jonah, the Lambert Drive property owners are security staff for the GMO and LGKB. Seems like a pretty upmarket area for a security job wage. Fake?"

"Only in terms of where they work. My guess is they're security and key personnel for whatever this place is."

"So, if it *is* an underground complex, what room do we need to hit?"

"That's a good question." Angel turns away and walks over to her laptop. She calls up a map on the screen and sits staring at it in silence.

Okay, so let's think about this. The smaller rooms could be offices or server rooms. If Angel wants to disrupt the city monitoring, they could be viable targets. If not, it'll be one of the bigger ones we need to hit. "It would really help if you told me what you want us to do down there. I might be able to at least guess at which room we're looking for then."

"We're going to *talk* to those in power. And I think I know how to find out where they'll be."

"Okay, how?"

"Dean Hollister and Jonah Burrell both bought land before the city was built. If we assume they were the first to do so, then we can take that as significant. Ethan said I'm aiming for the heart, which is true in a way. Taking it literally, though, where in your chest is the heart?"

"Less than an inch to the left of the middle of your chest."

"If I'm right about the placing of those properties, the third house up sits at the midpoint between Hollister and Jonah's homes. The middle of those plans and slightly to the left...here."

She places a finger on one room in the house. It's not the largest room, nor one of the smaller ones. "That's as good a guess as we're gonna get, eh?"

"I think so. I want to be certain of a few things before we make a move though."

"Such as?"

"I know at least one dealer tunnel comes out close to Lambert Drive. I want to see how close, so we can see if that's viable as an entrance point. I also want to find some definite evidence we aren't being sent on a wild goose chase."

"Makes sense given the risks. How do you propose we get that?"

"We're going back to Jonah's. Tonight. Don't worry, we're going to stay back and watch from afar. Good old-fashioned surveillance."

"Is that wise? After our break-in, Jonah could have bumped up security."

"I'll make sure we have some Sweepers at our disposal, just in case. So, go rest or do whatever you would normally, and meet me back here at seven. It should be dark by then."

*

I was glad to see Angel had obtained another car for us to use, rather than stick with mine. If nothing else, I don't want the police to spot me and come knocking just yet. I'm still nervous though. I'm not entirely certain I can trust everyone in the King's Guard. And Angel? I'm not certain she even trusts me fully.

The little metal box Angel has on the dashboard crackles and a voice comes through. "Coming up now."

We both turn to the West of Lambert Drive, watching through infrared goggles. Sure enough, three human shapes appear from the ground, just behind a house one street over. Angel presses down on a button on top of the box and replies, "We've got you. Spread out, check for security, and pay attention to anyone who enters the house. One of you check the power usage too."

"Roger."

Angel relaxes back into her seat and lets out a sigh. "I told you before I wanted to instigate change, but I wasn't sure how much yet. I think I know now."

I nod. "That's good. I know I'd rather walk towards potential death with a clear idea of what I was dying for."

She laughs. "I know I'll have to deal with Casille. That'll be interesting. It'll be the closing of a chapter for me too. He's the easy part of all of this. I knew New Hopeland had secrets, but with everything we've uncovered, I'm not stupid enough to believe I can take over."

She waves her hand vaguely in the direction of Jonah's house and continues, "This is way too big for me. When you really think about it, there's only one reason the city is being run the way it is. Crime is out of control, so the government are taking back control without the criminals knowing. They're letting them all live in ignorance; unaware their lives are not what they think they are. So, why do it just here?"

I sit back now too and stare up at the stars. It's a clear night. "It's a test. New Hopeland was built as a living trial."

"Exactly. People like me? Our days are numbered. I'm pretty sure California will be one of the next targets. I want to change that. I want to show them I'm too much trouble to tackle directly, and then use my knowledge as leverage for negotiating."

"No, that's not right. You may not have told me everything you've been thinking, but you've tackled this aggressively when it's come to direct threats. You want us to break into a secret government complex and find the people in charge. That's a physical confrontation, not a negotiation."

She shrugs. "Confrontation is the only way in. This system they're running is set up that way. Besides, I'm sure Casille wants to close things off with me too. He'll enjoy our meeting. It'll be cathartic for him. Aside from that, I'm hoping simply showing them what I'm capable of will be enough. And if not? At least I'll go out in a blaze of glory. That seems fitting."

"And how exactly is that supposed to leave me in a better position than I started in?"

Angel reaches out and pulls a small disc out from somewhere on the steering wheel. "I know you've been secretly transmitting things to the King's Guard for a while now. I was running security and caught one of the signals coming from Bert. This is a scrambler. The light goes red when it's blocking a transmission. It has been green all night. Given your gargoyle is on the roof of the car, that can only mean one thing. You removed the transmitter from Bert, didn't you?"

"I destroyed it."

"Part of me expected to have to win you over tonight. But then I noticed you didn't bring Bert with you when we started researching the housing boom or checking the plans. That means you have solid doubts over whether the way the city is run is right. That's why telling you about my aim for negotiation is risky."

"Because it means you're embracing this to an extent."

"Exactly. I'm not so foolish as to not see the advantages, even if my choice is born from a corner I've been unexpectedly backed into. So, let me make you an offer. Once this is done, you can join me in California. You'll still be a PI, still fight the good fight, and still have a direct link to the criminal in charge. The difference is, I'll give you more control over the relationship. I won't play games like Casille does or make veiled threats. Of course, I'll expect you to take particular cases for my benefit, but in return, I will deal with those who were too careful to allow your methods to be effective. Give and take: you scratch my back, I scratch yours. Simple. Lori can come too; there's a huge Tech Shifter community in California."

"You're trying to sell me the same corruption I'm struggling with now."

"No, I'm asking you to accept corruption to a lesser extent."

"I'll be honest with you, Angel. At this point, I don't know who to trust. If this was an attempt to win me over with the truth, you've made a misstep."

She looks at me and smiles, far more gently than I've seen her do before. "Catch-22. If I don't tell you, you don't trust me. If I do, it means trying to get you on board with something you'll hate."

"Honesty is still better. Tell me this then. If you knew I was transmitting to the King's Guard, why didn't you block the communication before?"

"I needed them to think they had an advantage. They needed to believe they had someone on the inside. Really, they did. You wouldn't have gone to them if you were always on my side in this. That's part of why I was cagey around you. They got snippets, but not everything, and will have been left with an incomplete picture. The potential that I was on to them, and the belief they still have an asset who's close enough to me to be useful. If I blocked the transmission tonight, it would give them confirmation I found the transmitter, and I'm getting ready to come in, nothing more. Winning you over was important overall because pulling the safety net out from under them will be key.”

“You had a lot of faith in getting me on board with your thinking, didn’t you?”

“I was more confident when I thought a takeover was viable, but yes. In a way, you started all of this, you know.”

I turn my head to look right at her and frown. “How do you figure that?”

“Some of the things Eddie Redwood’s software pulled from Hollister’s records made it onto the net. I only noticed because, by then, Gary Locke’s ideas had started to leak out in the wake of his trial. I was already interested in New Hopeland from a purely business standpoint, but what he said made me think there was more going on than I realised. I’ve been in contact with him on and off since then. Were it not for Gary Locke, I would never have learned that Malcolm Castleford had uncovered something, and so would not have come here quite so soon or in the manner in which I did. Gary Locke was sent down because of *you*, Cassie. Malcolm Castleford too. You are the one constant in the chain reaction that lead to me making a move.”

“I’m not sure that makes me feel any better. Locke and Castleford were important too, and they’re both dead.”

“Fair point. Look at this like a game of chess. Me and Casille, we’re kings. We both need other pieces around us, because you can’t play with a king alone. Gary Locke and Malcolm Castleford were pawns. They moved slowly and in set patterns. You, though, you’re more like a knight. You’re difficult to control, but you have a much more diverse mode of attack. That being the case, I’d be far more reluctant to use you as a sacrifice.”

“Reluctant, eh? That’s not the same as guaranteeing not to put me in danger.”

“There are things I’m certain about, Cassie. I trust the way you act enough to be sure you’ll make the decisions I think you will, for example. But in the end, there’s only one guarantee I can make with absolutely no doubts. When this is done, I *will* get what I want. That’s all there is to it.”

The communicator box crackles, and a voice comes through again. “Jonah just opened the front door and let someone out.”

“His wife or kid?”

“No, a male.”

"Infrared showed only Jonah and his family inside," I reply.

"Agreed," the Sweeper says. "We've also been watching. He appeared inside the basement."

"I've finished with the power consumption check too," says another Sweeper. "Those cables are hefting *a lot* of power. Far too much for one house of that size."

"Okay," Angel says. "That's all I needed. Sit tight and wait for further instructions." She takes her finger off the button and turns to me again. "I'm going to get one of the Sweepers to take me back. You take this car and leave it in the car lot where we picked it up from. After that, I recommend you talk to your girlfriend, just in case this all goes wrong. I'll send you your instructions when I have everything locked down. Tomorrow, we move."

*

The front door to Lori's bungalow clicks and opens, leaving a slightly surprised Lori to greet me. "Cassie? I wasn't expecting you tonight."

"Sorry. I know. Can I come in?" I hold my sports bag up to show her. "I have clothes for the chest of drawers."

"Someone's eager." She giggles. "Sure, come in. Go on through, I'll put the kettle on."

I nod and follow her in, shutting the door behind me. Lori branches off into the living room so she can get to the kitchen, and I make my way to the bedroom. A quick look around shows I was remembering correctly; there are no cameras here. Or none I can see. I'm still playing this safe. It took me a while to get here tonight. As well as dropping Bert home and packing the clothes, I needed to get a lot of stuff noted down.

"So, come on, what really brings you here tonight?" Lori asks, entering the room. She walks up behind me and leans around me, spotting the little note I've placed on one of my shirts:

Don't react, just keep talking. Read the note on the NHC Blend.

I pick the shirt up, revealing the phone, and start gathering similar items. "What can I say? I figured you'd be missing me already, so thought I'd drop by."

Chapter Eight

I'm in a darkened room, sitting at what appears to be my worktable. Sitting opposite me in the void is someone I could really do with talking to right now. He smiles that Chow Yun-Fat smile of his and greets me the way he always did ever since I was little. "Hey, Cass."

"Hi, Dad."

"Good day?"

I smile and shake my head. "Not really, no. What about you?"

He looks around at the never-ending darkness and replies, "Can't complain, all things considered."

A tear runs down my cheek. "I miss you."

"I know. Things are getting tough, aren't they?"

I let out a little laugh and wipe my eyes. "I can't complain too much; this all my fault. Some things never change, eh?"

"Even if you can lay the blame at your own feet, your intent is always the right one. Remember that."

"I do, it's just...I've always thought no matter how far into the darkness I go, I'm always heading towards the light. Where I'm at right now, I'm not sure there is a light anymore. No matter how I look at it I'm backed into a corner, and the only way out that doesn't guarantee *everything* coming to an end is to side with the biggest manipulator I've ever met."

"Hmm, that is a tough one." Dad sits back in his chair and crosses his arms. "You asked me once why I stuck with the PD when it was so corrupt. Do you remember what I told you?"

"That sometimes, the only way to instigate change is from within."

He nods. "And if you can't change the things that are wrong, then being on the inside is the only way to keep things under control. There are times when the only thing good people can do is perform damage control."

"These days, I'm better at damage creation, I think."

"To be fair, you always were. I liked to look at it less as destruction, and more moving things out of the way."

"Maybe I should have worked in the construction industry."

Dad laughs and gets to his feet. He beckons me to do the same and then turns me to face away from him and places his hands on my shoulders. Ahead of us are two open doors. One leads to a hallway bathed in a bright white light and the other is in complete darkness. "It's time to make a choice, Cass."

"How do I know which is which?"

"You already told me the answer. Trust your instincts."

I take a deep breath and exhale. "Okay. Okay. And Dad? Thank you. This helped."

He loosens his grip on my shoulders and steps back. "No matter what happens, remember this: I'm proud of you, Cass."

Without looking back, I step forward and walk through into the darkened hallway.

*

I slept well and woke up resolved in my course of action. I know it wasn't really my Dad, but he was right. I already knew what choice I had to make. What choice I'd already made.

The day went by in a blur and only seemed to slow when Charlie came to my door. "You ready?"

"As I'll ever be," I reply, stepping out of my apartment. "Angel hasn't told me the plan yet though."

Charlie looks around to make sure nobody is obviously listening in and says, "Wait until we're below ground and I'll explain."

We walk in silence until we reach the dealer tunnels she guided us through before. Then, she explains. "She was certain you'd join us but knew there was still a little bit of doubt. She didn't want to give you your instructions via message just in case you decided to side with Casille and let him know what was going on."

"I considered it. That was my original plan. A lot has happened since this started though."

"I can believe it." She sighs. "You're not going to tell me what you two uncovered, are you?"

"No. If this goes wrong, not knowing will keep you safe. Or safer, anyway. If Angel's plan succeeds, then you'll find out anyway."

"In that case, I look forward to us celebrating with a bottle of honesty."

"So, what are we doing?"

"The plan is that you, Angel, and five Sweepers are going to enter Jonah's house and find your way down to the floors below. Angel said you know which room you're aiming for, but she'll be leading the way anyway. Once you get there, she'll take care of negotiation. You're there as a familiar face. She trusts you to step in and take control of the situation if negotiations don't go well. Plus, you're tough enough to survive." She pauses. "Oh, and she said if things go how she expects them to, you'll have a simple task to accomplish."

"Which is?"

"She said you'd know what to do when it happens."

I glance at Charlie and, when I realise she's serious, ask, "Are the Sweepers up to date with what's going on?"

"They're hired guns, so no. They know they're working against a man named Casille di Franco, but not who he really is. Interesting aside, though, these tunnels were built with the blessing of the Four Kings. In that respect, us Dealers have always had a link to the Kings. Or one king as it turns out. After today, we'll see who holds the power."

We arrive at a small ladder and Charlie points at the hatch above. She lowers her voice to a whisper and says, "This is where I leave you. Angel and the Sweepers are above ground, watching the house. Listen. I know you. Far better than Angel does. What you said about keeping me safe? I'm doing the same for you. Whatever happens, trust that, and trust what I'm certain you're planning to do, okay?"

I nod and silently climb the ladder. When I push my way out into the light, Angel helps me up out of the hole and says, "I'm glad you came."

"In the end, there was really only one choice I could make. Still, eleven seems a little early for this. Should we be going in at night?"

"Jonah's wife and daughter are out right now. At night, they'd be home. I'm trying to keep casualties to a minimum. The last thing I need is another revenge-focused person coming after me. I have far too many of those already. You have your Glock, right?"

"And plenty of magazines."

"Good. I don't see Bert anywhere."

"With the way he is, I thought he might complicate things."

She nods. "There's some lightweight body armour behind that rock over there. Slip it on and we'll head in."

Sure enough, Angel has supplied me with a sturdy vest. It's a good fit too. Once I'm dressed, we head down to the house and Angel once again uses a less than subtle round of kicks to break the front door open. This time, the Sweepers go in first, moving with a highly trained precision as they cut alarms and check out rooms before we enter. The door to the basement is unlocked, so we head straight down.

On first glance, it's no different than you'd expect. Boxes piled in corners, cobweb-covered things under dust sheets, and even a rack of expensive looking wine are all present. Knowing which way the complex extends make it easy to find what we're looking for. A large crate sits against one wall and, when examined closely, has a set of hinges hidden on the side. A couple of hard pulls, and the front of the crate swings open, revealing a door at the back with a call button on the side.

Angel presses the button, and once the elevator arrives, she gives her first order of the mission. "Two of you stay put up here in case anyone comes in. The rest of you come with me."

I follow her into the elevator, and three of the Dealers' mercenary task force step in in front of us. They turn and train their guns on the doors as they close, and the metal box starts to descend below ground.

*

The elevator stops with a bump. "That didn't take long."

"I guess they didn't build it too far underground," Angel replies and hits the button to open the doors.

The three Sweepers fan out into what appears to be a simple waiting room and make a show of checking the doors for obvious watchers. Once Angel and I make it into the middle of the room, they turn in unison and point the guns directly at us. For the first time, I take in the fact they're carrying assault rifles. *Great. How is* this *protecting me, Charlie?*

Angel smiles and leans closer to me and then whispers, "Here we go."

"No chatter," one of the Sweepers says. "On your knees, hands behind your heads."

We comply, and he lowers his gun to use his radio. "Okay, you can head down now."

"Roger," comes the reply.

The clear leader turns to the security camera in the far corner of the room and says, "We've got them, Mister Di Franco."

The elevator noisily starts heading back up, and Angel rolls her eyes. "So, how long have the Dealers been planning to turn on me?"

"They didn't turn on you," the Sweeper clarifies. "They were never really on your side to begin with."

"I see. I don't suppose I could buy your contract, could I?"

"Once a contract is signed, it cannot be outbid."

"I thought so. Shame that."

"Enough talk, Tanner."

The elevator stops back on our floor, and the doors slide open.

Bang. Bang.

The bullets slam into the lead Sweeper's head, and he falls back slowly, discharging his rifle as he falls. Lucky for us, his bullets hit the ceiling alone.

The other two Sweepers react slower than I expected, and before they can get a clear shot, each has an LV on them. The masked assailants slam the mercenaries against the wall and, in an almost choreographed motion, bring their guns up to their foes' chins and pull the triggers in unison.

The Sweepers drop to the floor, leaving a streak of blood to mark their trajectory down the wall like a macabre snail trail.

Angel gets to her feet first and checks out the assault rifles. "Fingerprint locked. Ah well, we'll have to stick with what we have. You can get up now, Cassie."

I realise my arms are, embarrassingly, still behind my head and drop them to my side before standing up. "The two Sweepers in the basement?"

"Dead," one of the LVs replies.

I eye our saviours and then turn back to Angel. "Now what?"

"Now we keep moving. This way."

Angel checks the door opposite the elevator, and once she's certain the coast is clear, she starts us off on a run through the halls. Being the last through the door, I just about make out the sound of metal landing on metal somewhere inside the elevator. *Stay close, Bert.*

We make our way into another room and stop in our tracks, barely avoiding the bullets that land in the floor in front of us. At the back of the room, Devin Carmichael and Sunglasses Paloma stand guarding a door, guns raised and pointing our way. For all the familiar Southern edge to his words, I can't help but shiver at the coldness in Devin's voice as he states, "That's far enough."

The two men step forward, and in a flash, the LVs have moved to meet them. Angel shoves me to the side, and both of our masked colleagues succeed in disarming the scariest men in New Hopeland before taking aim and firing off a series of shots. Neither Devin nor Sunglasses are so easy to kill, though, and manage to duck under the guns and lay into their assailants with punches and throws.

Angel grabs my shoulder and drags me back out of the room, telling me, "We'll go the long way."

"*Diu.* Who are those two?"

"Efficient soldiers who screwed up in a major way and almost got me caught back in California last month. In truth, they likely won't be able to kill Devin and Ethan, but they will definitely keep them busy. Live or die, their debt to me is cleared."

"Did they know who they'd have to fight?"

"Of course. But they also knew it was this or I finish them myself. That would be a much slower process."

"If you expect them to lose, then doesn't that mean you're expecting us to have to deal with Devin and Ethan ourselves?"

"No. All we need is time. Make it to the main room, and I win. I'm certain they'll place the heads of the project there just in case I have intel as to their location. It's a logical way to try to control my actions. Those people are likely indispensable to the project. We take them, and we have leeway for a safe exit."

"That seems a bit..."

The sound of metal landing heavily cuts me off mid-sentence. Up ahead, Donal O'Brien tears around the corner, wearing full anthro TS gear. Time slows for me as he charges forward, and I notice Angel dart forward, pulling something off her shoulder as she does. As Donal dives at her, she drops into a slide and launches the little metal box at him. It magnetises itself to his TS gear, and the next thing I know, there's a large flash of light and the sound of electrical static blasts out. I slow long enough as I pass to see the smoke rising from his suit and then speed up again to come in line with Angel.

"That leaves one more," she says, and sure enough, as we pass an open door, Lieutenant Hanson leaps out and barrels me into Angel.

We all hit the floor, and when Angel catches my eye, I mouth, "I got this." She nods and scrambles to her feet and then runs on. Hanson starts to do the same, and I lunge, dragging her back to the floor.

"You stopped transmitting to us," she says, fighting to get on top.

"I know."

Hanson pushes me back and rolls to her feet. I stand up far less gracefully but manage to draw my Glock and point it right at her. She looks at me and says, "I have faith you're not doing something stupid. Or not more stupid than normal, anyway."

"I wish *I* did."

"It doesn't have to go down this way, Cassie. You can still make the right choice here."

I sigh. "There was only ever one choice I *could* make." I swing my gun upward and shoot out the lights above Hanson, causing her to turn her head away and guard her eyes. That gives me the chance to dash forward and swing a hard right into her head, dropping her to the floor. I look down at her unconscious body and say, "I'm sorry," and then run to catch up with Angel.

She enters a room, gun drawn, and I hear her say, "Hello King."

I slow to a stop and, pushing up against the outside wall, sneak towards the room. When I look back over my shoulder, I have company. *It's now or never.*

Turning quickly, I enter the room and bring my Glock up. I aim it straight at Casille di Franco. He hears the movement and glances over his shoulder. I notice the confusion on his face as he starts to back up, moving his gun between me and Angel. *I have to time this right.*

"Where are the others?" Angel asks.

Casille smiles. "Once they knew what was going on, most of them scattered to safe locations. I'm one of the only Council members left in the facility."

"That's fine," Angel replies. "You were the main one I was after anyway."

"Is that so? You do know I wasn't the first to hold this position, don't you?"

"Lower the gun, Casille," I say, keeping my voice low.

He looks at me and I flick my eyes over my shoulder. He follows and, seeing we're not going to be alone for long, backs himself to the semi-circular table taking up most of the back end of the room. "This isn't a kill the ruler to assume their spot sort of role. Disposing of me won't change anything."

Angel shrugs. "This was a show of power more than anything. But now I know you're not the only one here, I can indulge myself a little. I do so hate leaving things unfinished."

Bang.

My shot catches Angel in the knee, and she drops, turning the gun towards me as she does so.

With a loud roar of, "Caw," Bert leaps from his position on the ceiling and lands on her arm. His weight forces her hand down as she pulls the trigger. Bert clamps his beak down on her hand and, with a loud rip, launches the gun across the room, bringing two fingers with it.

Angel lets out a guttural scream and clamps down on the remaining stubs with her other hand, trying to stop the flow of simulated blood. Quick as a flash, Casille is in front of her, his gun pressed to her head. She turns to face him and starts laughing. "You won't kill me, Casille."

"No?"

"No. See, I know there are two reasons you never kill anyone yourself. One is to avoid getting your hands too dirty to keep up this charade of yours. The other is that you can't. You aren't like me or even the detective over there. For all your power, you don't have the stomach for it."

Casille smirks and replies, "My father did though. He was smart too. That's why you killed him, wasn't it?"

"Exactly. I'll be fair; he never once begged for his life. He died as well as anyone who has ever opposed me. But die he did. By *my* hand."

Casille's eyes glaze over, and I swear I can feel the temperature in the room drop. "You're right. I could never kill another living person. I've seen enough of that over the years. The thing is, you're a machine. You're not a person."

"Ah."

Bang.

Angel's head snaps back and her body follows. She hits the floor with a *thud* and turns her head to face me, synthetic blood pouring from the open wound. "You really don't disappoint..."

Bang. Bang. Bang. Bang.

Each successive shot removes another chunk of her face, until all that's left is a vaguely human shell, electrical sparks flying from the remains as it lies in a pool of red liquid. It's not the same as real blood. Not when you're looking for differences.

"Seven, nine, thirty-one, D."

I know that voice.

"Caw." Bert slips into a standby pose.

"Jonah?" I say, but as I turn my head, something hard hits me.

Just before everything goes silent, I hear Casille yell, "Wait!"

*

Light.

Bright enough to hurt.

I groan and cover my eyes, forcing myself into a sitting position. Slowly, the room comes into view. I'm sitting on a very basic-looking bed. The only other things in the room are a toilet and sink. Inspecting the door, I realise I'm in a cell. And my head is still hurting from whoever hit me. "*Diu.*"

Outside the room, I hear someone say something muffled, and seconds later, the door opens. Hanson steps in. She sits down against the wall, watching me. "I've changed my mind," she says, rubbing her head. "My advice to Lori is to not piss *you* off."

I nod at the locked door. "Bit much, eh?"

"Yeah, I told them this wasn't necessary, but that decision was above my pay grade. Still, it could have been worse. If Casille hadn't stopped Jonah..." She shrugs and then says, "Anyway. Can I get you anything?"

"The time would be a good start."

"About six in the evening."

"I've been out for a few hours then."

"Yeah."

"Any chance of coffee, dinner, and the key to this cell?"

She smiles. "How about coffee, half a chicken sandwich, and nice try?"

"That'll have to do. You lied to me though. About the King's Guard."

Hanson opens the door and waves at someone who passes her a mug and a plate, which she, in turn, passes to me. "No, I didn't. I may have danced around your questions over the years, but I've never once lied to you. I make a point of that these days. Now Donal, he told you I wasn't KG, so he *definitely* lied to you. If you see him, feel free to take it out on him."

"Is Donal okay? I thought…"

"He'll be fine. Whatever that thing Angel hit him with was, it was effective. He's got a few burns that'll need some time to heal, and I've not got a clue how he'll explain it to Hoove, but he'll recover. It's weird though."

"Weird how?"

"The box had multiple settings. Any of the top three would have killed him. I don't get why she didn't go all out. She's never seemed like the sort to underestimate people's strength."

I chomp down on the sandwich and take a mouthful of something that smells very caffeinated. "Can I ask you something? Without you dancing around the answer."

She shrugs. "I owe you that at least."

"Angel told me you killed Casille's mom. Is that true?"

Hanson sighs. "This would have been back in early 2053. I was working for the police department there, but not as a full-time member of staff. I was sent to California specifically to track Angel down. All the department knew was I was aiming to capture her, and they needed to accommodate me. She was already causing them a lot of trouble, so they were more than willing to let me do what I needed to."

"Who were you tracking her down for?"

"Dean Hollister. He'd made some deal with the military, and the group I was part of decided I was a good fit for the job. He'd heard rumours about Angel, and after talking to Jonah, he knew an AI like that would be useful for his bigger plan. Jonah was happy to build him another one, but he wanted to try recovering Angel first. The best way to do that was to target one of her people. Arthur di Franco was a logical choice because he was a mid-level criminal at best but had ambition. If we could get close to him, that would give us a way in. The plan had been to work it so we could drive him upward and ride the coattails and then use him to get what we wanted.

"So, as soon as I got there, I went undercover. It became very clear, very quickly, that Arthur would not be an easy person to get close to. But, if he had one weak spot, it was his wife, Isabelle. He was devoted to her to the extent that he'd do anything if she asked. Isabelle, we were told, wasn't the most faithful person in the world. So, I worked my magic. She was in her late thirties and beginning to feel it. When a twenty-year-old suddenly started showing her some attention, she took the bait."

"Huh," I say. "I didn't realise you like women."

"I prefer men. And truth be told, Isabelle was a little too prim and proper for my tastes. It was a job, though, so I did what I needed to. Time went on, and I wormed my way in enough to start getting chances here and there to check files. The problem was, Isabelle was hurting. She'd begun to see a future with me, and we both felt shitty about it. Me because I knew I was leading her on, and her because the truth was, Arthur was a good husband. She hated what he did for a living, but he treated her well. She only slept around because he said he was fine with it due to his need to be away from home so much. Talking to her...she was a nice person. She just fell in love with a criminal. Then started falling for me.

"It got harder and harder to keep it up. She'd burst into tears at random times and start doubting whether she wanted to be around me and then spend hours apologising. In the end, *I* slipped up. She caught me communicating with my PD contact and flipped. I tried to calm her down, but she pulled a knife. I shot her. We were staying at a hotel at the time, and the whole thing was caught on the security cameras, so that was me done. I had to get out of there, fast. The hallucinations Angel showed me? Hotel footage. Like I hadn't relived the moment enough already. If I'd just been a bit more careful..."

"Does Casille know what happened?"

She nods. "He would have been eight when it all happened, I think. The thing is, she had a reputation for sleeping around. Even at that young age, he knew something was up even if people didn't spell it out for him. He was angry with me for a long time, especially when he heard the truth, but we worked it out."

"So, what happened to Arthur?"

"He figured out I was undercover and traced my contact. A little torture loosens lips, right? Arthur was efficient, I'll give him that. Long story short, he found me and Dean Hollister. He would have killed us there and then if Dean hadn't taken a risk and shown him some footage of Angel's early days. I think he thought we were nuts at first; he told us he pitied us and wanted us out of the city. He started seeing the signs, though, and within three months, he was working *with* us. He'd made it fit in his head that it was Angel's fault Isabelle died; if she had been human, I wouldn't have been sent in and so on.

"The plan changed then. He was going to find a way to take her down and come with us. He didn't know it, but he was going to step into the role Casille now holds. He figured out Angel was on to him and decided to throw himself at one big attempt on her life. He asked me to save his son first, just in case it went wrong. So, I got him out of there. You know how that turned out for Arthur."

"I just realised something. You were twenty back then...that would make you forty-six now."

"Yup, and I look great. Dev was surprised too. He's actually only a little older than I was when I went undercover in California. In a way, I'm surprised the gap doesn't bother him. I'm glad it doesn't though."

"You sure he isn't going to be another fly in Suzy Spindle Legs' web?"

Hanson looks down at her black widow spider tattoo and laughs. "I hope not. He's one of the good guys."

"Still, I never really considered people's ages before. Looking at the people involved with all of this, I'm beginning to wonder if I'm the only one in New Hopeland who doesn't have a magical ageing portrait in their home."

"Nah, you're just too self-critical."

"That so? So, you'd happily manipulate me into bed if you were undercover, would you?"

"In a heartbeat," she says, and gives me a cheeky wink.

Knock-knock.

The door to the cell opens and Devin Carmichael walks. He tips his cowboy hat at me and says, "Hey, darlin'. Glad to see you're awake. How's your head?"

"Fine," I reply, finishing off the mug of brown stuff. "Well, as fine as it can be after being knocked out."

"I can relate," Hanson says.

Devin smiles and offers Hanson a hand up, which she takes. "It's almost time."

"Already?" Hanson asks, and he nods. "I still think it should be..."

Devin cuts her off. "No, it shouldn't. And ya know that."

Hanson sighs and then looks over at me and says, "Well...good luck, Cassie."

I hold the mug up and reply, "Thanks for the coffee, Rebecca."

She waves in response and starts to leave, but stops dead in her tracks when what I said sinks in. She turns back towards me and asks, "Donal?"

"Yup."

"Okay, I'm letting you off this once. He's gonna get it though." And with that, she leaves the room, leaving me alone with New Hopeland's number one hitman for hire.

He reaches behind the door and pulls out a bag of clothing. "I grabbed ya some clothes from your place. Some wash stuff too. I know it ain't much, but the sink works fine. You'll probably want to freshen up. The Council wanted to speak to you in person, and trust me, they don't do that often."

I study his face for a moment. He's smiling the same smile I'm certain he shows his clients; all charm and all designed to make you feel comfortable. *Almost time, eh? Here's hoping this goes how I want it to.*

*

I give the cell door a knock to let Devin know I'm done, and he comes back in. He looks me up and down and says, "I wasn't sure what you'd want, so I went with what I'm used to seeing ya in. White shirt, black trousers, black tie."

"Works for me. Until this day is done, I'm classing myself as still on the clock. My work uniform fits the situation."

"It does that," he replies. "The Glock and your main phone will be returned to you when this is done. I don't think they're gonna give the NHC Blend back though."

"That's fine. I was going to turn it in anyway. Gives you a chance to see exactly what Locke, Angel, and I found."

He nods and pulls the door open again. "Shall we?"

"Not like I have a choice," I reply and follow him out into a hallway. Everything seems deserted. That makes sense given what happened, I guess. Speaking of which. "Did Sunglasses survive?"

Devin chuckles. "He's fine. Those two were...motivated, shall we say? But nothing Ethan and I couldn't handle. I'm sure he'll appreciate your concern."

"So how do you two know each other, anyway? Way back when you took me to meet him and Casille, I got the impression you went back a long way. Given the stuff I dug up, I doubt it's just a case of you meeting in the King's Guard."

"I guess there's no harm in you knowing that, under the circumstances. Remember the story Angel told ya about Joe? We were both part of that unit. See, until then, we had a bit of a rivalry. Who could take down the most bad guys, that sort of thing? That day though? It made me doubt things. I'd always believed no matter what we did, it was always for the greater good. We were the heroes, doing what needed to be done to keep everyone safe. I didn't take it as hard as Joe did; I kept going for a while, but I couldn't help but question things.

"Ethan, he took it all in his stride. He knew we fucked up, and he knew what we did was wrong, but to him, it was his job. Sometimes things happened, but overall, he was fighting the good fight. So, there came a time we parted ways. He stuck with it, I quit. Then, a short while later, Ethan comes to my door with a man named Dean Hollister. I'd become a postal courier, believe it or not."

"Really?"

"Hard to imagine, ain't it? I hated the job. When they explained what Dean had planned, all the fail-safes and things like that? They drew me back in. Truth be told, I never was much good at anything other than killing. So, here I am. He worked his magic on Joe too, obviously. It's funny, but Ethan and Dean both have that way about them."

"I assume Hanson wasn't part of the same team?"

"Nah, she came much later. And Dean found Donal somewhere; I never was sure where."

I look around, taking in the lack of change in personnel numbers. "I'm in trouble, aren't I?"

"Maybe," he says, without a hint of humour. "The Council appreciates what you did, but they also know how deep you dug. That don't leave them many options, darlin'. Still, it ain't a lost cause. I wouldn't have insisted on taking you to the meeting if it was."

"Okay, I'll bite. Why did *you* insist on taking me?"

"Well, this is gonna get tricky. I think ya knew that already though. Ethan is what I'd call *efficient*. One slipup, even slight, and he'd execute you on the spot. And let's be fair here, Caz. You are prone to saying the wrong thing at the wrong time. Hanson and Donal? They like you far too much. They know the risks, and there's a good chance you'd never make it to the meeting with either of them, simply because they'd find a way to let you go.

"Now me, I'm a bit more balanced. I like ya, Caz. And I have every faith ya can work your way through this. If ya say something stupid, I'll at least give ya ample opportunity to recover."

"But if I don't recover, you'll kill me," I reply, pointing out the obvious. "I think I'd have preferred Hanson to take me."

He chuckles. "Would ya though? Deep down, ya know how that would go. Sure, you'd be free, but you'd spend what remained of a suddenly very short life on the run."

"With friends like these." I shake my head. "How would Joe have treated me in the same scenario?"

"Same as Ethan. You may not have realised it, but Joe respected what you do. He trusted in the quality of your work, or he wouldn't have been willing to act the way he did. He *did* hate you though. I wouldn't take it personal by the way; he hated most people, even those he liked."

"And here was me thinking it was my charming personality. Okay, so what can I expect?"

"I couldn't tell ya for sure. But I'll give you some free advice; if they make you an offer, there are four possible answers ya can give. Only one of them doesn't result in death. You'd do well to look at it like a business meeting. In a way, that's exactly what it is."

"Four choices. Rejecting the offer has to be death. Accepting whatever they say should...no, wait. If I accept it blindly, that'll be the same, won't it?"

He nods. "They're businessmen. They like to know how to motivate people and keep staff happy. If ya were to accept an offer without question, they'd view ya as likely to do the same again for someone else. Maybe someone who stands against them under the right circumstances."

"Then negotiation is the key. Ask for too much and I'm a liability but make myself clear and I'm safe. That doesn't leave me much of a target to aim for."

Devin shrugs and stops at the door to the room where Casille shot Angel. "I never said it would be easy."

He opens the door and we enter.

Chapter Nine

The table I saw earlier snakes around three sides of the room in a semi-circle shape. Looking around me, I recognise Dean Hollister, Jonah Burrell, and Casille di Franco. There are six empty seats. I nod to them and ask, "Aren't we missing a few people?"

Dean Hollister responds, "Bar Devin, we don't need the King's Guard present for this. And sadly, Marie Chambers has to hold things together with the mayor today. She trusts us to make the right decision though. Please, take a seat."

He points to a single chair, placed in the middle of the room, facing the three people in charge of my life. I do as I'm told and notice something on Jonah's lap. "Bert?"

Jonah helps him up onto the table and explains, "He's in docile mode. Every Familiar built in New Hopeland has a unique vocal code to place them into it. Don't worry, I'll return him to normal once we're done here. And I'm sorry about the, ah, misunderstanding earlier."

"Misunderstanding?" Casille says. "If I hadn't stepped in, you would have shot her."

"I owe you my thanks for that," I say and then turn to Jonah and add, "And don't worry about it. You weren't to know."

Dean Hollister clears his throat and says, "I'm sorry, but I would rather not drag this out longer than we have to. Miss Tam, we know you've uncovered a lot of information about New Hopeland. Could you please, in as few words as possible, tell us what you think is happening here?"

"Does the NHC Blend summarize that?"

"I'm sure it will, yes, but we haven't finished analysing it yet. On top of that, raw data does not allow for differences in interpretation. So, please go ahead and tell us what your thinking is."

I cross my arms. "I think New Hopeland is some sort of test zone. You wanted to check the viability of asserting governmental control covertly. You secretly watch everything and have fingers in every pie the city has to offer.”

Hollister nods and asks, “And why do you think we are doing this?”

“To perfect the model before rolling it out across the rest of the country. Stretching the reach of the Four Kings further into the State was the first test of how easy it would be to control a larger area.”

“Quite so.”

I frown. “Can I ask you a question?”

“Go right ahead,” Jonah replies.

“The system means Casille, under the guise of the Four Kings, controls almost all the crime in the city, as well as a good portion of it in the rest of the State. But if this is all to assert control, why set up so much crime at all? Why not rein it in further?”

“Everyone is a bad guy on some level,” Casille replies. “Everyone has urges. To reduce the damage of crime and corruption, you don’t need to wipe it out, but rather control it. Those who are more inclined to break the law will do so regardless; this method just means they have an outlet without ever knowing the government is controlling what they can and can’t do.”

“It is a thinking we apply to all things,” Hollister adds. “The unsavoury rumours about local politicians? Most conspiracy theories you see pop up about the city? They are all us. People want to rebel; they want to feel distrustful. We allow them to do so without risking the normal potential outcomes.”

“Even with Casille not killing anyone,” I reply, “this must still all result in you doing things most would at least view as deplorable, if not outright illegal?”

“Much as you do,” Hollister says. “The ends justify the means.”

I nod. “Sometimes, good people can do bad things and still be good people after the act.”

Jonah looks at me and asks, “And you believe us to be good people?”

I run my hand through my hair and say, “I think you all believe you are, at least on some level. I believe you’re doing something messed up with good intentions. That’s close enough.”

“For what it’s worth, I understand how you feel about it all,” Hollister says. “New Hopeland was my concept, but I’ve had my doubts over the years. That it works is what tells me it was the right decision.”

"And was manipulating me into coming to New Hopeland the right decision too?"

Somewhere behind me, Devin laughs. To my surprise, Dean Hollister is also smiling when he responds, "I wondered if you'd figured that out. All things considered, I think it was. You've done a lot of good in this city, Miss Tam. Though I must confess, we were worried for a moment. Why did you destroy the transmitter we gave you for Bert?"

"Given how close an eye Angel was keeping on things, I thought it was likely she knew I was using one. The way I saw it, if she *was*, then destroying it would make her more inclined to tell me what she was planning. If I was wrong, then it wouldn't make a difference as far as me working with her went."

"You do realise you risked ending up the same way she did?" Casille asks.

"I did. Looking at it now, though, I don't think I would have."

"How so?" Jonah asks.

"Because I don't think you killed her."

"Nonsense. Her body completely shut down. I'd know; I designed it."

"I know that. But before we started the assault, I was told I had one task to complete but she wouldn't didn't say what it was, other than I'd know when the time came. She had complete faith in her ability to pre-empt my actions. Before she shut down, she looked at me and said I didn't disappoint her. She knew I was going to turn on her."

"That doesn't prove..." Jonah starts, and I raise a hand to stop him.

"Back when we broke Gary Locke out of prison, she took control of the LV suit I was wearing. She outright stated she could control a *flesh bag* from across the country if she wanted to. Then, there are the two LVs who tried to stop Devin and Ethan. She told me they were enlisted as a way of paying a debt. They screwed something up and almost got her caught back in California. She said that was last month."

"Last month? She's been here longer than that," Devin says.

I shake my head but keep facing the Council. "Examine the remains thoroughly. My guess is you'll find it wasn't her original body, but a copy she's been controlling remotely from California. That would explain what she meant when she said she took care of the tracking bots she had injected in her when she was playing Nurse Bridges too."

Casille looks at Jonah and asks, "Is that possible?"

"It...could be."

"Then we'll have to strike California."

"Not necessarily," I say, drawing their attention back to me. "Angel told me she wanted leverage. She wanted to negotiate. Her goal here wasn't to bring you down, but to show you what she was capable of and escape. As erratic as her behaviour was, I don't think she was trying to scare you into backing off. Angel told me with the system you're running here, her days are numbered. I'm certain she'll contact you. When she does, I recommend you listen to her."

"Oh?" Hollister replies. He drops his chin into his hands and watches me with an interested look on his face. "Why is that?"

"Think about it. You could probably bring the entire US military into play to tackle her if you wanted. But why do that when you can assert the same control over her as you have here? She may not be as compliant as Casille is, but if you can negotiate terms where you can place people there to guide her actions and deal with issues, you'll be able to expand the reach of the system. Even if it turns out to be a temporary arrangement, that has to be less messy than all-out war. It would also leave you with people on the inside if you ever did have to bring the relationship to an end."

"We will take that under consideration," Hollister says, a slight smile on his lips.

I sigh. *Here we go.* "Okay, look. I've told you what you needed to know, I helped with Angel, and I've given you political advice. Can we please get to the point of why I'm here?"

Hollister nods. "You were brought to New Hopeland because we needed to test a new variable. You see, while this is not technically a military operation, the ex-military personnel do still act as though it is, at least while on a job. You were someone from outside the system, but who has a moral viewpoint that, at its core, is compatible with our goals. So, yes, we made sure you got here, and have sent you the occasional case to make sure you stay here. We needed to understand if someone such as yourself could become part of the system.

"Joe Farrah was a sad loss. For all his faults, he was truly a good man. He was also our eyes and ears on the streets when the monitoring systems failed to find what we needed. While we *could* pick up the slack ourselves, it seems more logical to replace him. The King's Guard speak highly of you, and the work you have done for each of us has been impressive. As such, we have deemed it prudent to simply speed up our own processes and offer you his place on both the King's Guard and the Council."

"What would it entail?"

"In basic terms," Casille replies, "we will feed you jobs. When we need something checked, or a specific job carried out, it will fall to you."

"There wouldn't be any real change for you." Hollister adds. "In terms of your current work practices, everything would remain the same. You'd still be a PI, but one with ties to the system."

"I see. Mind if I make a few demands?"

"Please do," Jonah says. "We thought you might."

"Let's start small. I want the mortgage on my apartment paid off, and the annual fees covered each year I'm working for you. Fuel for my car would be nice too. I intend to work as a regular PI on top of dealing with your cases, but I want easier access to information and equipment when needed."

"The apartment, fees, and fuel are fine. And we wholly expect you to continue your general work. Your reputation in that field makes you so suitable to replace Joe. As well as the money you get from independent cases, you will also get a flat rate wage from us. It won't make you rich, but it will be liveable on its own. The only proviso is that the cases *we* send you must take priority. We can negotiate on a case-by-case basis, however. As to information, we expect you to continue to follow legal protocol, but we will expedite what we can. In terms of equipment, we will certainly help, but do not overdo it with your requests."

"Sounds reasonable. I also need to know what I can and can't tell my partner, Lori."

"Ah yes, Eddie Redwood's sister. We're making good use of the tools he created, actually. As to what you can tell her, I am afraid the answer is nothing. None of those within the system are permitted to tell their partners about what we do, and you will not be an exception. If you are simply worried that dating a member of the King's Guard will place her in danger, then I can certainly guarantee her safety. You can take that as payment for her brother's work."

"You're honestly telling me none of you go home, sit down with your partners, and say, *hey, guess what we orchestrated today?*"

"It's tough but necessary," Jonah replies, and I can hear the sadness in his voice.

I rub my eyes. "Okay. Okay, I get it. No telling Lori, but I'll take everything else."

"Good," Hollister says, offering me a handshake. "Glad to have you on board."

I rise from my seat and shake his—and the others'–hands. "What about the dealers? The Elites know about Casille, but do they know about any of this?"

"No," Casille replies. "The Elites are technically King's Guard now insofar as they know who plays the Four Kings. None of them dug as deep as you did though."

"In fairness," Devin adds, "we gave Caz here reason to dig. We didn't give the Dealers any extra hints to get them curious."

"I assume they *were* in on the plan to stop Angel though?"

"Ya got that one right, darlin'. You personally were never in danger from the Sweepers either. Us towards the end, but never the Sweepers. Charlie made sure of that."

"Okay. Hey, if I'm part of the Council, I'm not gonna have to attend regular meetings and work on city policy, am I?"

Hollister smiles. "The occasional meeting will be a necessity, I am afraid. In terms of decision making, you will be the same as Joe was. And the same as Devin, Donal, Ethan, and Hanson for that matter. We may sometimes ask for your opinion, but the ultimate responsibility for the project belongs to those of us in political positions."

"Good," I reply and nod to Bert.

Jonah says, "Seven, nine, thirty-one, D."

Bert stands up and, seeing me, clambers up my arm and onto my shoulder with a happy, "Caw."

"Oh," I say, "one more thing. This has all left me tired. I want two weeks off. Think you can survive without me for that long?"

Devin laughs again and says, "I think we'll manage."

"Good." I turn and walk out of the room. Glancing down, I notice the tie Devin grabbed for me has a deer embroidered on it.

Wealth and long life, eh? I wonder if he knew that when he picked it.

*

Somewhere in the back seat of the car, Bert trips up and lets out a flustered rattling of his beak. I glance in the rear-view mirror and watch him scramble back onto the seat. Meanwhile, in the front passenger seat, Lori turns her head to read a road sign and asks, "How far to the border now?"

"Not far." I smile and shake my head. "You're far too excited about this."

"I can't help it; I want to see where you grew up. Plus, I'm proud of you for reconnecting with your mom. It's silly, I know, but I can't wait to meet her."

"Yeah, well, enjoy the awkwardness. Still, with everything that happened, my savings are all intact. If things get *really* bad, I'll get us a hotel. Or I can feed her to Ink; that works too."

Lori gives me a playful punch in the arm and then says, "You're sure there's nothing in here listening in?"

"Yeah. I triple checked everything before we set out. Even Bert."

"Caw."

"See? He agrees."

Lori laughs. "Good, because I wanted to talk to you about what happened. That mouth communicator looked pretty painful."

"It wasn't too bad. I expect they'll become commonplace if the Council takes my advice and negotiates with Angel. As far as I know, it's not a model we have in New Hopeland."

"The earpiece was normal at least. The thing is, you letting me listen in at all confuses me."

Uh-oh. You know where this is heading. "Why's that?"

"I can overlook the danger it put me in. If someone had found it, then I could have destroyed the earpiece before anyone could trace it. For you though? If they'd checked in your mouth and found it, you were absolutely risking your own life there. Considering the position you were already in, that just seems...I dunno. It was way more risky than normal for you."

"Come on, how likely were they to check my mouth?"

"Seriously, Cassie, why risk yourself like that?"

My chest tightens. I steel myself and say, "Because...I believe you should be honest with the people you love."

I blink. I swear the clock on the dashboard is broken. No way was that one second; it was an hour, at least.

"I love you, too, Cassie."

"Caw," Bert protests.

Lori giggles and turns to face him, replying, "We love you, too, Bert."

"Caw," he says, and sits down again.

I snort out a short laugh and hope it's enough to stop Lori noticing the tear running down my embarrassingly blushing cheek. "Hey, once we get to Vancouver, do you want to find somewhere to stop for coffee? I don't know about you, but I could do with the wake-me-up kick."

"Sounds great. Keeps you driving safely, and it's a good excuse for you to stall seeing your mom, right?"

"Am I really that obvious?"

"Afraid so."

"*Diu.*"

The Cassie Tam Files Key Events Timeline

2033

Angel Tanner is "born" in California, built by Jonah Burrell as an AI prototype.

2046

Casille di Franco is born in California. His parents are the professional criminal Arthur di Franco and his wife Isabelle.

2049

Angel Tanner, now chronologically sixteen, starts asserting herself in the California criminal underworld

2050

Gaining a reputation for scary behaviour, as well as the ability to avoid identification and capture by the police, Angel Tanner effectively takes over the California crime scene.

2053

Rebecca Hanson is sent undercover in California in an attempt to investigate and take down Angel Tanner. The plan was facilitated by an entrepreneur named Dean Hollister. Her investigation meant manipulating Isabelle di Franco into a romantic relationship in order to infiltrate the organisation. Though initially successful, the plan falls apart when Rebeca is found out and ends up killing Isabelle. Arthur di Franco soon tracks her down and is made aware of Angel Tanner being an AI. He agrees to help, blaming Angel for Isabelle's death.

2055

Cassie Tam is born in Vancouver. Both parents are also Vancouver born, but her mother is of Canadian heritage and her father has roots in Pok Liu, Hong Kong, with his great-grandfather being an immigrant.

Arthur di Franco is murdered by Angel Tanner and the crime is pinned on Pauline Welch (later Mary Warner), who is sentenced to fifteen years in prison. Casille di Franco, then nine, disappears.

New Hopeland is founded, based on a concept by Dean Hollister. It is pushed heavily as the tech-focused city of the future. The original intent had been for Arthur di Franco to play a role in running the city once he had helped bring down Angel Tanner, but his death caused a shift in plans. His original role of the Four Kings of Utah was instead temporarily allocated as a role for the government agency in charge of the city.

Enforcement for the Four Kings of Utah falls to the King's Guard, a group of mercenaries who are assigned to dealing with issues that can't be resolved by public-facing means. The original three guards are ex-colleagues from the US military and consist of:

Ethan Cobalt, who works closely with the criminal underworld. He is cold in the way he deals with things, and approaches his job as just that, taking cases without concern.

Devin Carmichael, who assumes the role of a legalised assassin. He originally quit the military after an operation left him questioning why he did what he did. As such, the role allows him some autonomy in what cases he takes.

Joe Farrah, who became a gun shop owner and acted as an on-the-streets informant. He was previously in intelligence for the military group, and holds himself responsible for the operation that caused the group to originally split.

Dean Hollister, now in situ, starts work on the Tech Shifter concept.

2056

Lori Redwood is born in New Hopeland.

2060

Though not a new concept, VR business picks up in New Hopeland. Within a year, the two levels of VR Junkie are fully established.

Rebecca Hanson is brought into New Hopeland. She is fast-tracked through the ranks and soon holds the second highest position in the department, acting as high-end PD link for the King's Guard.

2065

Now nineteen, Casille di Franco releases a novel titled *Four Steps to Power*. He then emerges in New Hopeland under the name Allen Fuerza and, masquerading as a low-end criminal, assumes the role of the Four Kings of Utah that was intended for his father.

Pauline Welch is released from prison and returns to Angel Tanner in California.

Jonah Burrell is brought to New Hopeland and begins work on perfecting his AI tech concepts.

2070

Tourism declines in New Hopeland, as more cities start to adopt a similar aesthetic in terms of tech.

2072

Familiar Enterprises Ltd is officially formed by Jonah Burrell and work begins on the Familiar Project.

Cassie Tam, now nineteen, joins the police academy with the intention of following her father into the police force. She is ousted without passing, due to being unwilling to accept the corrupt end of enforcement, and her father helps her set up as PI.

2073

Cassie investigates a case the local police ruled as an accidental death. She discovers the perpetrator was a senior official in the local government and had used their sway to get away with murder. Though her father warns her off, Cassie continues to investigate and finds conclusive proof, leading to the official being arrested. The police release him on bail, and he breaks into Cassie's home. Cassie's father dies protecting his family, leading to Cassie and her mother becoming estranged.

Dean Hollister publicly announces the commencement of work on Tech Shifter gear. He also brings Donal O'Brien into the city and places him in the New Hopeland police force, under the agreement that Donal will eventually take the gear on board.

Ethan Cobalt is caught on camera after the death of a man named Johnny. This becomes the first case of a member of the King's Guard being shown in the news.

2074

After months of awkwardness, Cassie leaves Vancouver to start a new life in New Hopeland, cutting contact with her mother. She became aware of the city through online ads that were fed to her by the New Hopeland officials who had seen her work as a PI as a potential boon for the city. She sets up as a PI and buys an apartment, but is left with a large mortgage.

2075

Tech Shifter gear is made available to the public. The TS Murder Files are opened within one month, following a string of murders perpetrated by early adopters of the gear. These are government employed criminals, whose purpose is to create a sense of fear around the gear, making it not only more useful to the police, but more appealing to the military. Tougher protocols on who can and cannot use the gear is added to appease the public, though this was always the intent.

The tourism trade in New Hopeland is now officially dead, but the city maintains its strength in attracting businesses.

Tapper Gloves are invented and, shortly after, are licensed by the Four Kings of Utah.

2076

Carl Sanders changes his name to Gary Locke. He wishes to cut most ties to his father, believing his military contracts to be part of a larger issue, but keeps his old name for business purposes, hoping to use this to leverage information. He forms the conspiracy blog *The Roots of Eden are Rotten,* which expands to become a protest movement.

2077

Cassie Tam starts dating Charlotte Goldman, a licensed drug dealer, albeit one with a decent moral code.

The New Hopeland PD creates the Tech Shifter division, and Donal O'Brien is promoted to the position of Marshal for the unit.

Lori Redwood, sister of The Roots of Eden are Rotten member Eddie Redwood, undergoes the Tech Shift procedure, and acquires Ink.

2078

Cassie Tam and Charlotte Goldman split up. The relationship was a happy one, but they drifted apart over time.

Though unnamed at the time LVs—Light Vampires—first appear in California.

2079

Cassie Tam investigates the disappearance of Jonah Burrell's daughter. When she finds her, he pays her with Bert, a Familiar unit in the form of a gargoyle. Bert is unusual in that his programming is a hybrid of the common Family and Protector class units.

Vancouver-born William Deveraux, aged twenty-five, joins the New Hopeland PD. He immediately clashes with Cassie Tam, but the two work through the issues.

2080

Flesh and blood animals now account for only one-third of pets in New Hopeland, with Family class Familiar Units being more popular.

Cassie Tam is hired by Lori Redwood to investigate the death of Eddie Redwood, uncovering a clash between Gary Locke and Dean Hollister. This results in Dean pushing forward quicker with certain plans. After the case, Gary Locke is imprisoned, and Cassie and Lori begin dating.

Cassie is hired by a Tech Shift performer named Kitsune, and is tasked with finding their missing dog. During the case, Cassie is drawn into a conflict between Allen Fuerza and his accountant, Malcolm Castleford. She meets Ethan Cobalt for the first time, and learns that Fuerza is actually named Casille di Franco and is also all of the Four Kings of Utah. Malcolm Castleford is imprisoned.

LVs turn up un New Hopeland, and attack Cassie, amongst others. Forced to work with the PD and act as bait to draw them out, Cassie learns a little more about the King's Guard. She discovers the LVs are led by Angel Tanner, and she is aware of Casille. During the case, Cassie also finds out there are three hybrid programming Familiars, Bert, a human-appearing woman Angela Faraday who works for Jonah Burrell, and a third, unnamed unit. Though Angel escapes, her associate Dr Sanderson is imprisoned.

Devin Carmichael admits to Lori Redwood that he has helped pull some strings in Cassie's favour before now.

Cassie is hired by Dr Faraday when she is stalked. During the case, Cassie learns that Jonah Burrell's home street, Lambert Drive, was rumoured to have been intended to have more houses. Once she uncovers Angel Tanner as the stalker, she also learns she was the first hybrid programmed Familiar unit, and Angela Faraday was a contracted creation. Angel kills Frank Tyson, an associate of Gary Locke, and ensures that Dr Sanderson kills Malcolm Castleford in prison. She gives Cassie enough of a hint that something is wrong in New Hopeland to entice her into considering a partnership. At Lori's behest, Cassie reaches out to her mother to mend bridges.

Cassie sides with Angel Tanner in order to find out what is happening in New Hopeland. Cassie soon learns that Rebecca Hanson is in the King's Guard, and she starts to unravel the origins of the city and Tech Shifter gear. Cassie reluctantly helps bust Gary Locke out of prison, but after he discovers that Angel is an AI, Angel executes him.

Cassie attempts to help the King's Guard take control of the situation, but Joe Farrah is caught up in a gunfight and is killed by Angel Tanner, leaving Cassie is a difficult position. Charlotte Goldman then shows signs of siding with Angel, causing Cassie to make a choice as to how to proceed. During a raid on the secret unit under Jonah Burrell's house, Cassie turns on Angel, and Casille di Franco is able to kill Angel. Cassie is knocked unconscious.

When she awakes, Cassie speaks with Hanson and Devin and is able to fill in some blanks. After negotiating with Dean, Jonah, and Casille, she joins the King's Guard, replacing Joe Farrah as their eyes and ears on the streets. She then takes a holiday, confessing her love to Lori and taking her to meet her mother.

About the Author

Matt Doyle is a speculative fiction author from the UK and identifies as pansexual and genderfluid. Matt has spent a great deal of time chasing dreams, a habit which has led to success in a great number of fields. To date, this has included spending ten years as a professional wrestler, completing a range of cosplay projects, and publishing multiple works of fiction.

These days, Matt can be found working on multiple novels and stories, blogging about pop culture, and plotting and planning far too many projects.

Email: mattdoylemedia@hotmail.com

Facebook: www.fb.me/MattDoyleMedia

Twitter: @mattdoylemedia

Website: www.mattdoylemedia.com

Other books by this author

The Cassie Tam Files

Addict

The Fox, the Dog and the King

LV48

Shadows of the Past

Also Available from NineStar Press

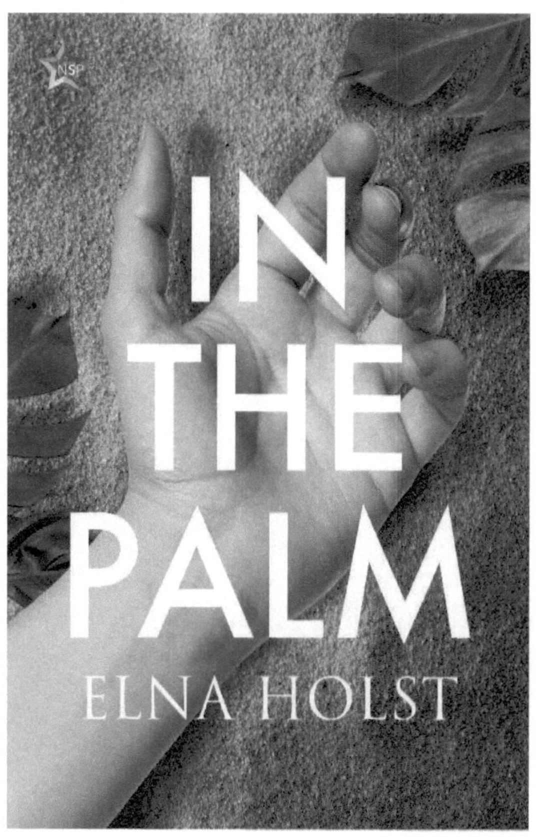

Connect with NineStar Press

Website: NineStarPress.com

Facebook: NineStarPress

Facebook Reader Group: NineStarNiche

Twitter: @ninestarpress

Tumblr: NineStarPress